Leitus and Ben Ymir found themselves face-to-face with a giant wrapped up like a mummy.

Long arms reached out to grab Ben Ymir, who struck a blow to the giant's crotch. With a noise that sounded like the laughter of hell, the giant lifted Ben Ymir effortlessly off the ground.

Ben Ymir then tossed his dagger straight into the giant's chest—where it accomplished nothing. "Next," rasped the unnatural voice to Leitus, "you will tell us where the witch and the boy are to be found."

Leitus grabbed the magic sword he had brought from Rome and stabbed at the giant's eyes. The being flung Ben Ymir aside, shrieked, and reeled back through the door. . . .

Ace Fantasy Books by Richard Monaco

BROKEN STONE
RUNES

RICHARD MONACO

ACE FANTASY BOOKS
NEW YORK

BROKEN STONE

An Ace Fantasy Book / published by arrangement with
Holy Grail Co., Inc.

PRINTING HISTORY
Ace Original / January 1985

Cover art by Boris Vallejo

ISBN: 0-441-08134-7

Ace Fantasy Books are published by The Berkley Publishing Group,
200 Madison Avenue, New York, New York 10016.
PRINTED IN THE UNITED STATES OF AMERICA

For Darsi Adele

and

"Ennie"

ANTONY

Noon. Shimmering heat. The sand was almost pure white between the road and the flickering horizon. The shadows of the palm trees lining the wall pooled close to the trunks.

Marc Antony half dozed in the saddle, rocking slightly with the slow clack-clack of the hooves on the paving. The sun was a hot, brassy weight on his shoulders and skull. He'd taken off the helmet and looped white cloth over his head. He sweated steadily.

Egypt, he thought, vaguely. *Maybe this was all a mistake. . . . How much farther can it be?* Because they'd told him at the last town that the river was ahead. A branch of it anyway. A short ride. The dark natives in their loose, cool white robes had watched him and his men, wordless, as they rode into that blazing sun-shocked noon when no sensible creature stirred from the shade. They had already learned that Romans were not sensible.

His face throbbed with sunburn. He should have waited. . . . His escort was perhaps fifty yards back now, wilting in the terrific heat. He was gradually losing them.

I should have retired after he died. . . . He meant Caesar. *I can no longer tell if these things are my own will or fate alone. . . . I am like a man who marches in a drifting boat . . . I move as I please and arrive nowhere. . . .*

He squinted into the furnace of hot breeze and blunt sand. Thought about her now. Wondered what he really felt. Remembered her with a kind of cool distance. Remembered how they'd parted. Was it even remotely practical?

Yet there's no other way to go but backwards. And can Antony go backwards?

By the time he turned upriver his men had straggled 200 yards behind. The sun was halfway down the sky. His shadow stretched out behind him, man and horse one exaggerated shape.

He was having trouble focusing on the war that was following him. It seemed absurd: one man being followed by a war. All those men, legions, marching irresistibly to destroy him . . . and her, of course, except she could make a pact with them. But wouldn't because of pride and folly and the dark stream that carried them all along to dark doom. He sighed.

Cleopatra, he thought. *Ah . . . and I am not Caesar and I don't want what Caesar wanted. . . .*

Yes, he had his woman and had inherited his ambitions. And all he wished now was that he could go home, that he had a home.

I have to win an empire or nothing because there's no middle road for me anymore . . . what a joke . . . and I don't want to win an empire. . . .

He wondered how the twins were, his children by the Egyptian queen, who was Greek. What would they think of him in times to come when he was dust? He hated the way men were remembered by the living. A few words. A summary of so much effort and hope and pain: a few mere words to cover the inexplicable and total passions of a human life. He sighed.

I could tell myself to win it for my children, except why lie and lie in the face of doom?

His eyes hurt from the unrelenting sun-glare. But he

had to push on. The bronze death machine was at his back. He could imagine them, glittering like beetles on the sun-blasted sand, grinding after him.

"I'm tired, Egypt," he muttered.

His lips were dry. He took a slug of brackish water from the skin that swung at his mount's flank. It helped.

I have to recover my stomach for it all . . . concentrate on strategy. He nodded . . . then drifted into images of his twin sons and their subtle-eyed, translucent-skinned mother. Egypt herself. Greek Egypt. *It's going to be hard seeing her again* . . . he thought. Because he'd deserted her, gone home and married a Roman. She would have done the same, he believed, if their positions had been reversed. To protect herself, or worse.

They'd made love for days at a time. He remembered everything, even the drunken parts, when they'd lied and hoped and made great plans together. She hadn't wanted him to go. He'd known that but blocked it from his mind.

He pulled his brain back to war.

Avoid a sea battle at all costs, he reasoned; as at Actium. Let the legions chase the Egyptians across the empty sands to weary themselves. Yes, Sound, as far as it went. But sooner or later they'd have to stand and fight, and the Egyptians simply didn't have the battle skills. *Chase us until they drop . . . or we do.*

He was still thinking about it at sunset, coming to the pyramids at Gizah. The immense shapes cut the reddening sky, wrapped in silence. The Sphinx was on the far side, invisible, lost in shadow.

The outlines made him think of great teeth chewing sand and darkness. Cleopatra had once told him they had never been tombs. What then? She'd shrugged. They are knowledge itself, she'd said.

His horse was fagged. His sitbones hurt. He needed to rest and drink, eat. He looked behind for his men. The road went back in a dim curve and lost itself in the gathering shadows. How had he gained so much on them?

He shrugged. He knew there was a well close to the Great Pyramid. His troops would find him there. He kicked the weary animal up the slope as the band of dark red clouds across the horizon deepened as if clotting.

He couldn't locate the well. It was completely dark. He gazed at sugary, crusted looking stars in the moonless sky. He'd forgotten how huge the pyramid was.

He dismounted and walked on the lowest stone terrace. He chewed hard bread and cheese from his saddle pack and washed it down with saddle wine.

A remarkable thing, he thought. Cleopatra had said there were hidden entrances and passageways, and that the structure could change a person who entered and teach him the history of the future. The structure itself, she'd insisted, affected the human mind and soul. He'd smiled then; but standing here, he wasn't smiling. There was no humor in awe. The very vastness of it looming over him brushed aside his ordinary thoughts; it was like a mountain cutting into the night's starry brilliance.

He paced and tried to plan again. Sighed. Rubbed his face. Kicked the massive blocks thoughtfully. Paced and ended thinking of nothing, gazing at the clustered stars, himself a mote lost in immensity. . . .

Stillness. . . . He walked along the stones and memories came unbidden. He remembered a smooth, lovely, delicate face. Found the name: the slave girl who'd been a Briton princess—Bita. Then recalled Leitus Sixtus, and all the incredible events came back from over a decade ago. Violence and magic, swirling madness, the crucifixion of Leitus, his escape—with Antony's help and the big gladiator. What was his name? . . . Lost it. . . . He'd been too busy to remember them for years now, and there'd been no trace, none at all.

What had happened? he wondered. *Those days changed me more than I cared to admit. . . .* He'd lost something—something he might have called simplicity.

After Caesar's murder he'd planned and counter-planned and fought very well, but something was always missing, even in the midst of action and victory. Yes, a part of him remained detached and looked on all the turmoil from a distance because once, fighting for Bita, it had all been simple. His motives had died and he'd simply acted because there was pain and shadow and he'd wanted to help. So he never gave himself completely to his purposes and triumphs. His fortunes rose, but he knew the end, felt the end, the canker in the blooming rose. He knew he'd fail for all Cleopatra's intensity and his genuine love. He knew he would fail in the end yet lived without saying so, which made him, he sensed, a man.

He remembered the one on the cross—the first one, the father of Leitus, when Antony was a boy himself. Spartacus the rebel hanging in a line with thousands of other slaves along the stone roadway, nailed at the end of miles of suffering after the rebellion that had nearly shattered Rome.

He levered himself up until he was sitting on one of the huge blocks and looked meditatively across the faintly luminous desert.

"What became of them?" he murmured. *And why had I forgotten so completely?* "Visions and gods on earth?" He smiled. Wondered. Shook his head. *A time of dreaming while awake, I think.*

His life had closed over it.

He sighed. More images: a scene in his villa garden.

Nonsense, he thought, remembering the mellow late afternoon sunlight poking through the grape arbor where he'd just been repulsed by young Bita. He'd stolen her from the villainous murderer Iro Jacsa and had decided to enjoy her that day. She'd done (he now believed) something hypnotic to him. A shock to his nerves. And then a strange and beautiful boy and girl had surprised them there and he'd been impressed, somehow, with the notion that they were supernatural beings. *Nonsense.*

Other memories: a soothsayer dying in the thunderstorm at Iro's villa . . . himself and his troops melting away, pursued (he later decided) by shadows and fancies wrung from the wild night, by lightning blasts and general terror. . . .

"Nonsense," he whispered, leaning back on the massive block—except there was no massive block, which shocked and tensed his stunned body. He frantically kicked his legs like a teetering babe, trying to rebalance and sit up . . . failed and went over backwards, clutching at nothing. *Impossible,* he thought as he dropped, hit a ramp of slick stone, and sped down an almost frictionless surface. He understood, far back in himself, that the time of dreams was upon him again.

Even that remarkable smoothness scorched his skin with speed until he got himself balanced on backplate and leather. He fell as in sleep far into the utter, silent heart of that immemorial stone.

He slowed about the time his armor was hot enough to burn him, and finally skidded to a stop in some deep, lightless chamber. He lay there on his back for a while, breathing and wondering about being alive.

All right, he told himself, *you just fell into the Great Pyramid. Why should that worry you much?* . . .

Finally he stood up and groped a little. Saw false light when he smacked his forehead on stone. He wasn't especially claustrophobic, but this was an extreme test of calm. He tried not to think about the rock over his head. Breathed deep and felt his way around the cool walls. His head throbbed like a drumbeat.

He kept himself moving slowly, one arm out in front, the other lightly scraping along the passage wall. After a stretch of time he couldn't measure, the way bent and he had the impression of a faint golden glow up ahead. Sunlight? Impossible—how long could he have been down here? The idea was a shock and tended to further disorient him.

He went on, blinking and straining to see. Another bend. The glow didn't seem to illuminate the corridor, which curved steadily now, in closing circles. That meant it was spiraling into the center, like a whirlpool in stone.

A faint hint, a shimmer, and he followed. Yes, down and down in a definite spiral. Tightening. He hoped there would be an underground passage out to the surface. As the turning tightened he kept thinking: *Suppose it just ends?* He'd just go back and try again. If there was a way he meant to find it. *Is this the end of Antony?*

Except he didn't really believe it yet. He still felt set apart, protected, supported by the force of destiny, like an invisible riverflow carrying men like himself through life.

The simile reminded him he was thirsty. He wondered if the stones would be damp. He'd heard of men trapped underground during sieges subsisting on such moisture, painstakingly collected.

The passage narrowed; now his shoulders were scraping both walls at once. He had to twist slightly to keep going. His heart sank.

A little farther and he was sliding sidewise as the perfectly smooth walls closed in.

Saturn and Io, he thought. Then his skull clipped the passage roof. Hurt. He cursed emptily. Had to stoop now. *A way for rats and mice. . . .* He considered going back but had less heart for that. A few yards of steep curve and he was down on hands and knees. There was just room. Now he'd have to back out. Sighed. His mouth was dry. *No more . . . no more of this . . . like being born in a stone womb.* His heart raced; his lungs strained in gathering, reflexive panic at the clammy air. His sweat was chill, as in sickness.

He was on his belly now, inching forward, the curve so tight, his body bent around it, scraping elbows and knees raw. He knew he could never withdraw now. He was done, doomed. He pulled, wriggled, kicked himself along. Felt his breath clogging his chest; felt dizzy; felt death close and stifling, its jaws gaping to swallow him.

CLEOPATRA

The Nile was still, smooth, polished-looking in the mellowed beams of the setting sun. Dark blue stained reddish gold.

The royal barge was moored near shore. Rich lacquers and giltwork glinted. Clouds of burning scent drifted across the perfect water.

The queen stood thoughtfully by the bow rail, facing downstream, where the shadows were filling in the details of the landscape. She thought something moved along the shore. An animal, perhaps. Something quite large, a blot of darkness.

A slim shaven-skulled boy stood at her elbow, deferential, careful. He was practically nude, barefoot. She wore a loose and flimsy robe over a sketchy tunic.

There were serving girls and sleek Nubian guards amidships.

"He'll come," she said, staring out across the water.

"For love, my queen?" he asked, voice trying to be neutral.

Cleopatra didn't quite smile. "For love, yes. Among other things, young priest."

"I pray you, do not mock me, my queen."

"Are you not still a priest?"

He sighed, watching her, hopelessly absorbed in her.

"I don't know what I am now," he said.

"Please," she murmured, "I am sad enough. Don't make it worse."

"What else can I do? At least if you're sad you'll think of me."

"I think of you, Naiar."

He rubbed his pale, fine-boned face with long fingers. "You think of me."

She turned and touched his arm, softly as a breath. He didn't react.

"Yes," she said. "And I'm sorry."

He snorted and moved just enough to free his arm.

"Spare me that at least," he said.

"I understand."

"No, you don't."

Behind them the palm trees tilted and bent along the flat line of embankment. The evening died into stillness and scent.

"Very well," she said, "I don't."

"The omens say . . ." he began.

"Yes?" She half listened, turning away again to stare into the suddenly limitless depths where the gathering darkness consumed the solid world.

". . . that you will be . . ."

"Yes?"

"Undone."

"Say to the end," she quietly commanded.

"They say this."

"That I will be undone?"

"You and the Roman." He managed to say "Roman" without quite spitting.

Yet she wasn't actually focused on him. Her pale, luminous eyes were absorbed, inner and wistful, catching the last hints of the day's slow death across the sheen of the water's surface.

"Me . . . and the Roman," she said.

BRITAIN

The slim, dark-haired, deep-eyed girl had just turned fifteen. She was walking alone, dressed in a pale tunic, climbing the steep, rocky slope among massed firs and twist-trunked yews. The path she followed was well worn, threadlike, overhung by the heavy, scented branches.

As she crossed the tree line she came out on the crest of a moundlike hill. Wooded, misty fields spread out below in the fading sunset's darkening reds.

She held a short stick—a wand really, wound with pale night flowers—in her left hand. Her bare feet were noiseless on the resilient, grassy, late-summer earth. She was chanting under her breath, softly, as wind whispers.

The hill went almost flat on top. A circle of massive, squared, broken stones crowned it. She stopped at the border and waited, facing where the full moon was about to rise. She knew where to stand so that the silver-white disc would just fit between two squat pillars where they intersected the horizon.

She knelt. The warm breeze rifled her hair. She waited, dark stare focused inward. The chant flowed softly and steadily from her.

The sun was down. The shadows lost their edges and pooled. The preternaturally luminous moon was just nicking into the space between the stones. There was a circle in the center of the stone structure, low-walled like a well. Two bearded druids, one lean, the other round-faced and balding, stood near the rim.

They'd been waiting for her and now looked up to face her. She was outside the stone perimeter, perhaps fifty paces away. The lean one whispered to the balding man:

"By what authority is a female admitted to these mysteries, Orl?"

Orl paused and pursed his full lips. He blinked nervously.

"Himself," he finally murmured.

The first raised thin, uneven eyebrows.

"Ah," he said. "That's it, then."

"Are you minded to debate him?"

"Ah, I'll leave that to you."

"And there's more," whispered Orl into the soft windsounds and the gathering pulse and murmur of insects. A string of fireflies crossed the bend of pillars.

"More what?"

The long, bearded head leaned closer to the ground. They both watched the slim girl now kneeling just inside the circle of stones.

"More strangeness." Orl rubbed his head with one soft-looking hand. "Tradition counts for nothing since—" His voice was barely audible. "—*they* got involved in things."

The other nodded, grave, uneasy.

"That's so, that's so."

"They say the masters have marked her for wearing the circlet."

"No surprise, brother Orl," he said, breath hissing out.

"The moon's here, the lady shines."

They stepped in unison to the rim of the well, which was like a cup of blackness sunk in the grassy earth. Orl was thinking bitterly about the general injustice and barely paid attention to the ritual steps of the initiation process: first, the approach to the holy pit; second, the song of awakening; third, the charging of the wand; fourth, the command to the lord of the world; then a drink of fermented herbs and the slow walk back to the village. He only sensed something was wrong when she reached the command, holding the little baton out over the pit as the rising moon was framed at the top of the stones.

She was supposed to say: "Lord of the earth, come to my aid in my need."

He didn't realize the strangeness until the full shock struck him a blow in the pit of his stomach. The light, contralto, teenage voice suddenly filled with thunder, and the words it cried out made no sense:

"Graaa laaa tho'm tho'm, Aataatana!"

Something like chill wind seemed to swirl in the pit and spill out in a cloudy puff that might have been smoke, smoke that teased their imaginations with the hollow outline of a face.

Orl's hand came out from under his robe with the dead, skinned hare in his hand that had been meant as meat for the mock sacrifice to fulfill the ritual of initiation. Nothing was supposed to happen. He never believed anything really would. His secret religion was nothing but form and politics. *Nothing was supposed to happen.*

Over the mounting howl of whirlwind that sucked at them, tugging their robes like snapping banners, dragging them to the lips of the abyss, they heard the immense voice and perceived that the stick in the girl's slim hand was flaming red, its color gleaming in the huge, shadowy face that now shaped within the smokiness above the pit.

They suddenly understood in a rush, both of them, that there *was* going to be a sacrifice. A voice boomed that couldn't have been the girl's alone:

"Take them, my father. Heed thy daughter, Morga. Take them! Take them for thy joy!"

And like leaves swirling down a storm drain, the two priests spun, tumbled, and were gone, in a shriek and flutter, into blackness.

Morga stood very straight. Her eyes were dreamy, her face serious, edged like a sharp blade. Her tunic fluttered in the wind. She whipped the wand in a waist-high arc and turned her back in a gesture of absolute command. The milling smoke and gale subsided. Then she turned and went quietly away, following the exact track she'd walked coming.

Outside the rim of stone blocks stood another priest. He was small, soft-looking, with one arm missing at the shoulder. His single big, puffy hand held a long staff. Standing almost motionless, head slightly cocked, he squinted as if even the moonlight was too bright for him.

"Well done, child," he said. "Did you feel strong?"

"Yes," she said, muted, remote. She'd been trained since an infanthood steeped in shadows and whispers. She'd had no playmates in the village, and only priests for companions. They didn't quite shun her, but mothers told their children to steer wide past her. Her earliest memory was of waiting in some musty hut, watching the mud boil in the street under the sheenless lead sky. She remembered leaning over the window ledge, the light, cool autumnal spatter flicking her face and thin arms. A woman's voice had sounded behind her, from the adjacent room, the sound flattened by the steady downpour dinning on the hide roof, words that hinted real meaning to her only years later.

". . . or else they'll sink her in the bog by law."

Then a male voice, blurred, resonant:

"Under the protection . . ."

". . . not responsible. . . . I am not—"

"We know, old woman."

". . . bog . . . or burned for worse. Her mother . . . Damned priests!"

"Say nothing of her mother."

"Before her birth dead, taken dead from her mother."

"Say nothing."

"Cut her out from the dead, living in a corpse all that time, the cord dry—"

"Is that all, old woman?"

"All what? All I saw?" Fear. There had been fear in the voice.

Then the male voice whispered; she had no memory of his words.

"Not me, not me," said the woman. "It were priest

Sarnac who called her abomination, not I. . . . I—''

''You ought not to have remembered.''

And the noise, the cry, commotion, flurry of thumps. She had turned and faced the hide-hung doorway, stretching her little legs down until her bare toes took the weight, then weaving over in a post-infant stagger, small hands struggling with the thick door hangings, blinking into the wet, musty dimness where a long, angular shadow (she didn't know was a priest yet) stooped over a heap of rags. She didn't realize it was her nurse lying there until he tugged the gleaming steel from the body; then the shock of comprehension hit her and she fled into the front room, turning at bay to watch the leather curtains part as the tall man stooped through the narrow doorway.

''Morga,'' he had said, His face seemed just a long nose under the dark hood. ''Child.''

The scene often came back to her in an uncertain memory of rainroar and old wet smells and childhood panic . . . a hissing voice saying: ''Daughter of the power. Beloved keeper of the earth's kingdom. You are safe now, child. You are safe.'' The glistening blade was the clearest image in the scene.

There were other images, too, blurred years, huts and caves, nights in the forest, torchlit rituals. Always training and loneliness and things that were never explained.

''Abomination,'' she said now to the one-armed priest at the edge of the stone circle.

''What's that?'' he asked her.

She shook her head slightly, lost in recollection, trying to find some substance in the gaps and shadowplay of long ago.

''Why must I do these things?'' she asked.

He cocked his soft-featured face, eyelids flicked open, showing blank, blasted eyes, lenses and white melted together.

''You don't know?'' he responded, tapping his staff on the earth.

''No. I do not.'' She paused and he waited. ''I should have been left to die.''

"Die," he said, snarling or smiling. "Die? You, who grew in the womb of a lifeless mother. Of whom it can be written that her father was darkness and her mother death?" He arced his arm from right to left with the staff as if the gesture confirmed something.

"You cannot die. There is a mate for you."

"So I can bear a worse thing than myself?"

He tilted his small head closer, as if to look up at the slight girl, and whispered like a grater on stone.

"So you will be fulfilled."

All her life there had been hints and rituals and blood. She shut her eyes. She'd known nothing else. No family or ordinary friends. And death all around her, covert and sinister. She'd been so trained in death, she barely reacted to it.

She didn't quite hate them all yet. The dark dullness of it left her empty.

There was no expression in her face as the dwarfish priest spoke again, tilting his unbalanced body left and right as if beginning to writhe around his staff.

"I really don't care about the kingdom, whatever that is," she informed him, "and I don't care to mate with anyone."

"You're still a child," he assured her.

"No," she said. "I'm not. I'm not anything."

"Have I not raised you like a doting father?"

"I'm not anything." She wasn't looking at him.

He squinted, averting his face from the moonbright.

"Your true father," he whispered drily, as if it might excite her, "will soon communicate with you. Yes. You will feel his touch." He nodded and twisted around the staff.

She blinked and didn't look at him, staring down the silver-shadowed slope into the blurred valley.

"Whom must I kill next?" she wanted to know.

ANTONY

He was trapped like an animal. He struggled to crawl past the next few feet of narrowing tunnel and then was stuck. When he tried to back up, he realized the sides had been shaped with sharp edges facing rearward so that when he tried to wriggle in reverse he jammed fast. A trap.

What an ass am I, he muttered, unable to go forward or back, sweating in the dankness. *I'm too fat,* he told himself. *I'm going to die in here.*

He twisted by fractions, trying to ease the paralyzing cramps. If he let himself relax, it was just bearable. But it was hardly bearable to relax.

At first he cursed and raged, even wept with fury and frustration. Later he dozed, stretched out in the utter blackness. He was never sure when he actually woke up because the dreams kept flowing past him in an unbroken ribbon—vivid, feverish dreams. Time melted . . . sometimes pain and chill . . . sometimes a soft, velvety touch . . . sometimes the terrible, pressing blackness—then the brightness of dreams. He'd find himself walking under the pyramid, wandering naked and cold down dimly luminescent corridors. Then he'd shudder and find himself locked in the utter dark again, and he'd reach with desperate greed for the dreams that were the only relief because his body was stuck fast and dying like a caught beast.

At some obscure point he dream-wandered up into a big chamber where an empty tub that resembled a coffin sat. A single sliver of moonlight seemed to be lighting it, and the pale light seemed to gather the glow into a subtle female shape standing in the stone container—a perfect shape of melted tones that faded whenever he tried to concentrate on the actual outlines. He had a sense of immensity, as if some inexplicably vast opening yawned behind her, something his consciousness quailed before.

The wispy shape wavered as if holding steady against some swift, unseen current. Words that weren't words and pictures and feelings that eluded the grip of his fevered awareness seemed to flow through him as if the speaking were in himself and yet came from outside, from her.

You, was somehow said, *must*, remote, intense, austere, *help*, soft, warm, honey and wine spilling over white blossoms, *him*, a boy he'd never seen in a misty, gale-swept landscape wearing strange armor, holding a long barbarian sword on his knees in obvious prayer. Images flowed like terrible, wonderful music, and he somehow realized he was only perceiving the dullest levels of the immense clarity and intelligence that was communicating so gently with him, trying with awesome tenderness not (he sensed) to rupture his (by comparison) fragile self. What she told him was the halation of her own perfect substance, not words that went out and were lost. He sensed faintly that the same, in a duller way, might be true of human beings as well, that even the sounds they made were truly a part of their substance—which gave a startling impression of what a curse or a lie actually was.

He now understood that he was in a vast machine of initiation that select acolytes had passed through for ages, often leaving their bones in the torturous, lightless corridors . . . pinned there until the bodies were worn down enough to let the soul show, so that she could communicate. He understood that he'd been prepared for this almost fifteen years before by the appearance of that supernaturally beautiful couple who had seemed to shape themselves from sunlight in his garden in the Roman suburbs when he had failed to seduce slim, lovely Bita, the slave girl. Later the terrors had struck at him on the rainwild grounds of Iro's estate and he'd fled, lacking the power to fight back.

You, she told him in echoes of images past, present, and to come, *were,* a stern but loving mother-feeling, *too,* music and softened sunlight, *fat,* echoing, *Antony.* His name was a shock to him, all its meanings spreading like ripples through his new, vast consciousness. Her voice that was not a voice went on:

Go, a songsinging, *to,* in mellifluous glory so that all heaven sang and trembled, *Judea.*

And he was back in the tunnel, stuck in his gasping, cramped, racked set of bones. But he found he could force himself forward this time, and he inched and twisted ahead, kicking, pushing on, on, until there was date-sweet, water-scented fresh air in his parched face.

Then he was blinded by unbearable brilliance. He squinted as he crawled, averted his head, struggling straight for the light, scraping already raw knees and elbows. The burning spot seemed far away down the narrow tunnel, and so he was shocked when his head cracked hard against stone. Blood ran into his eyes as he peered out a pinhole in the block straight at the sun. He didn't know it yet, but he was facing east and it was morning out there.

Still trapped, he thought. *This is some mockery of the gods.*

He slammed his palms and forearms wildly against the stone and was amazed again when it swung outward smoothly.

He pulled himself out and dropped ten feet into soft, warm sand and the oven-hot, brilliant desert day.

He swayed to his knees, feeling giddy and light as a feather. *How long have I been inside?* he asked himself. He could see his ribs, his sunken stomach.

His problems—meeting Cleopatra, finding his lost men, preparing for the onslaught of his enemies—seemed infinitely distant. He was held rapt by bright blueness and the sunimpact on the horizon of sand broken by lines of shockingly green date palms that blazed like bright metal cut-outs.

"Judea," he muttered. He should be trying to organize his forces, trying to hold the doomed empire together. . . . He remembered all too vividly the defeat at Actium, which had cracked their seamless dream. His troops were deserting and the Egyptian forces at his disposal would be no match for the legions. Why had he fought at sea? He was no admiral. In his sleep he still saw the burning ships and heard sailors' screams. Defeat . . . defeat . . . defeat . . .

"Go to Judea. . . ."

CLEOPATRA

Although her immense golden barge was moored at the quay before her palace in Alexandria now, she took her meals and slept on board. The rumor was that she was at all times prepared to flee the city.

The sun had just set behind Alexandria, the elusive violet last light glimmering, dying on the almost motionless surface of the Mediterranean. The tide turned. Her golden goblet was a glint in the shadows as she sipped her wine, seated alone at the massive table. The servants flitted silently around her.

He knew she was waiting for the Roman. For word. Any word at all. Ready to fly to him. She was sitting just far enough away so that Naiar had to raise his voice to tell her:

"The Romans will butcher your children when they come this time." He waited but realized she didn't even have to say "I'll send them away" because she really believed Antony was coming back with either an army or the power of the gods sitting on his shoulders. "He's gone," he said. "You know he's gone and left you." He saw the faint glint of the goblet again as he tried to focus on her outline—except the dusk had swallowed everything but the polished metal and the blur of her body. The stars were coming out, sharp and near. "The army will betray you."

He heard the clink as she put the goblet down. Behind

him the wind washed over the murmur of the city. He believed he could almost smell their uncertainty. Soon they'd be among Octavian's legions.

"Yes," she said, finally responding.

"Meaning, yes, you know."

"Yes," she repeated.

"Make terms with them or leave tonight, my queen."

She didn't even have to say "No."

He held one tensed, trembling hand to his face, breathing too fast, tears burning him, his despair and hopeless longing burning too.

"They are going to destroy you," he said. "They are going to destroy everything."

A pause. In the hushed evening he heard faint splashes, creaks, as the craft swung slightly on its moorings.

"You should leave the city, Naiar," she told him quietly.

He laughed harshly, almost savagely.

"You know I cannot," he said.

"You should. I could command it."

"You know I cannot," he repeated.

JUDEA

"You're in danger," the short, black-bearded Jew said, scratching himself under his coarse, woolen, shawl-like garment. He'd just come out of the dark side alley into the close oil-lit apartment.

He crouched in front of a rude wooden table. The smokey lamp sat in the center. A lean, serious man with light eyes and blondish-brown hair—a Roman, though he didn't look it—leaned forward on his stool into the dull rim of light that sketched his facial bones in shifting shadow. He gave an impression of terrific movement suddenly checked.

Another Jew, a rack of bones surmounted by a pointed face and greasy beard, sat up straight, tensed, stiff.

"Is this news?" the Roman asked, not moving at all, in a potent calm.

"Yes, yes, my friend," Arim Ben Ymir insisted. "And doom too. Doom." He shifted from foot to foot. He kept looking, deferentially, at the thin, desert-burnt man with a face like a knife edge, who clutched a long staff and gently leaned it against his creased cheek. His dark, violent eyes glittered as if nothing about his hungry shape was real but that stare.

"I've already met my doom," the youthful Roman said. He almost smiled. "We kissed and embraced."

This is the fatal year, he thought, *if anybody believes*

in fatal years. According to the prophecy. Here I live in the land of prophecies; here prophets make a market-place of wisdom.

"Leitus, they know about the holy weapon," Ben Ymir said. He was seriously frightened. Though the night was cool, there was sweat on his face. "That dog of a governor has ordered you be found and brought to him." He glanced, again, at the desert man.

"We don't worry about the Romans anymore," Leitus said.

"Hardar," said Ben Ymir, blinking rapidly, glancing left and right, whispering now. "My friend, Hardar, was slain in the street tonight. Yes. Yet no mark was found upon his body. They say the Angel of Death walks abroad."

"Perhaps he was not slain?" Leitus suggested. "Why say so?"

"A thing, I tell you," whispered Ben Ymir, "a *dybhk*, a thing of shadows. Many have seen it. They saw it hovering over Hardar. He was stricken in the street called Narrow."

The tensed, tanned lath of a man leaned into the smokey glow, the staff tilted across his cheek.

"Shadowy, they say?" he asked.

Ben Ymir shrugged. "The eye, they say," the stocky man said, nervous, eager, "cannot fix its form. All darkness and—"

Leitus stood up.

"So," he said. "This is the year."

He'd expected it, yet it was still a shock. And the prediction stood that he would lose his son. He chose not to believe it. He thought about the sword he'd brought from Rome that was never Roman. These Jews, the secret Jews of knowledge, called it the holy weapon. The sword with the writing on the blade and the jewels in the hilt-setting—he'd sold half of those already, here and there, to survive. He'd kept his family alive for fifteen years. His son and wife. His wife, the seer. The secret Jews had taken to her, he reflected, like to a long-lost sister.

"No," said the desert man, "we cannot fight."

"I didn't say anything," Leitus pointed out.

"What can be hidden from the wise?" Ben Ymir said, looking at the older man with respect.

"You have to take the weapon," said the lean man, "and go to the cold and bitter place it came from."

"I'm sick of hiding," Leitus said. "What about the promised king? Won't he want the sword?" He wasn't quite mocking.

The stocky man rocked his head and shoulders in a rhythmical *daven*.

"He who will free Israel from the harsh hand of the oppressor," he intoned. "He who will—"

"That time is not come," broke in the other, tapping the staff on the brick floor. "Hear me, Roman and yet brother, the evil one will be drawn to that blade. It is the tooth that will bite him. It is the gripe in his bowels."

"Aiie," sighed Ben Ymir, crouched almost to the floor. The shadow of the evil one seemed, to him, to be stirring in the corners of the room.

"What about my son?" Leitus asked.

"Isaac," said the older man. That's what they'd named him, renamed him, "must stay with his mother."

Leitus thought about the last fifteen years since the boy's birth after they'd escaped the catacombs under the sprawling Roman villa where his dead lover and her brother had lived. Her brother, Iro, the vacant-eyed, paffy, pale, obsessive, twisted creature who'd murdered his sister and blamed Leitus for it. Leitus had had to flee into exile with the ex-gladiator Subius Magnus and the slave girl Bita—now his wife—losing her, fighting with Caesar's army in Britain, making his way back to Rome, discovering his real father had been the rebel slave Spartacus. He had led his own rebellion, going down to defeat faster than his father—and ending crucified like his father along the Appian Way. Pain and darkness had drawn him from his body halfway through the door of death, and he'd been saved to fight a strange battle in the underground chambers with Iro and assorted demons and devils. Unchaining Bita, who was nearing her term with their son, and escaping with her from the blood and terrors with a special sword that was now called the holy weapon by the Jews, he'd never come back from exile.

All I wanted was peace, he thought. *A place to raise my son.* He winced. *Now it's found me again.* The terrible shadows, the fire and blood and terror.

The fierce-faced desert man stood up. His stare blazed without focus.

"We all have roles," he said. "Yours is to keep the weapon from vile hands. The Jews might lose the weapon to the evil ones."

"What's this?" asked Ben Ymir. "Would you betray our people?"

"Power will not unseat the Romans, much less the real enemies." The lean man shrugged. "A time is at hand when all power shall be set at nothing save the force of the Lord God of Hosts." His eyes shut and his voice went deeper, soft yet fierce. He had their full attention.

"Who are the real enemies, then," asked Ben Ymir, "if not the Roman devils?"

"Shadows," said the other Jew. "And only the true light of Israel can melt the shadows from the human heart." For an instant Leitus was reminded of something from long ago, his childhood—the feeling of springtime, the wonder and scents of new life. "That light, I say, knows neither Jew nor heathen. Though it comes from our people it does not belong to them, any more than the sun is theirs because it shines on them, for it shines everywhere the same."

Elsewhere, not many twisting streets away, Leitus' son, Arturus, now called Isaac, and his mother, Bita, were seated on the clay floor of a low-ceilinged chamber. An oil lamp sputtered where it hung on a thin chain.

Dull orange light and soft shadows fluttered softly over the slight, copper-haired, lovely woman in white and blue robes. The boy was strong and serious, wide in the shoulders. He wore a rough grayish woolen garment and sandals. His nose was long, with the faintest hint of a beak. His eyes were pale green and luminous.

When the thick plank door was strained open and a Hebrew priest came in, there was a flash of a dark corridor and the sound of distant chanting voices. This small structure was part of a stable leaning against the city's chief temple.

The priest adjusted his snowy beard as he went to his knees before them in a controlled, majestic movement that was not quite obeisance.

"Greetings," he said in Hebrew. His nose was a fierce jut, his eyes harsh, defiant, and shrewd.

"Greetings, Abram," said Bita, in the same tongue.

"They will soon betray you," Abram told her.

"Yes," she said. "I know that."

Her son understood. He'd had very little childhood. Oh, he'd played in the sands, climbed walls, swum in the great river on brilliant mornings, learned to ride camels as well as horses, ate sweet fruit at evening, tossed pebbles at wild dogs and chased other children through the clamor of the marketplace, robes flapping, sandals slapping. Only a few knew he actually wasn't a Jew, because he wore the clothes and hair and bent over the scrolls with the others. He'd been taught to read and learned the texts and prophecies and histories of Israel in the hot, clay-walled, straw-roofed classroom. He'd learned the feeling of oppression and the weight of Rome, and the uncomfortable feel of the collaborators, the friends of the occupation. But before he was ten years old, most of his time and energy was being spent in the hot, harsh hills with a sword and spear in his hands, his father teaching him to fight Roman-style. He'd learned to ride, charge with spear, fire a sling with the pinpoint perfection of a second David, whose story the boy loved to read and reread and retell himself and act out in the desert when alone, with a tree representing Goliath. The long evenings he'd spent with his mother and the priests while they trained him to sit perfectly motionless, so that later when he moved, something within him would remain still and strong and somehow apart from the rest of him—an inner calm that he would be able to call upon. Bita had believed it was only a trick of the druids in her native country, but Abram had said the wise in all nations had come to the same understandings—even to the knowledge of God, which they confused with names but recognized in the heart. Arturus had learned to sit on a stone in the blazing desert and not sweat, barely breathing, and feeling a strange, cool comfort well up like a spring within him. These were the things he'd spent his childhood struggling with, so that he was already older than most men in ways that mattered.

"You are not of our people, remember," Abram said.

"Neither are you," Bita responded, "if they but knew it."

"I issued from a Jewish womb, which is sufficient." His intractable, jet-colored eyes looked at Arturus, who thought they resembled dark stones just under the surface of a pond. "Young warrior," Abram said to him, "whose blood are you?"

"When I bleed," the fifteen-year-old replied, "it looks like all the others I've seen cut."

"Is not the unknown God just for the chosen?" Abram asked.

"Who can be sure whom God has chosen?" the boy responded. He knew this was an important conversation, though not why. "Why am I called 'warrior,' sir?"

"You'll learn in time."

His mother watched carefully. She was trying to be sure what the old priest meant. There was a hidden message in all he said and did. The truth of any parable could not be stated; its meaning changed for every case and viewer.

"Am I like David, then?" Arturus asked.

"David sang for God. Do you sing, boy?" The priest folded his long arms and tilted his head forward, seeming to study only the floor. Bita watched. *The floor is earth* was her thinking, *and the eye cannot penetrate it, yet we must not let it block our sight.*

"I won't let them have my son," she said. "No prophet or vision will sway me." *Am I refusing to see?*

The old man stayed bent over, his dark, blunt stare on the floor. The oil lamplight softly drew shadows around him.

"We can no longer help you, woman," said Abram. "You must read right or perish."

She knew there was no sense in pressing him. He and the other Kabalist priests would have made their decision, and there was no appeal.

"All right," she said. "What next?"

He didn't look up.

"You must leave the holy city. You must read your own fate."

"So you take even the seers of Israel away from us as well?"

"You are the seer, daughter. Isaac is the sword. And you will find what your husband is."

Daughter. She was touched. He'd never called her that before.

"Perhaps," suggested Arturus, "he is the one who will sing?" He smiled, but the old man seemed to take it seriously.

"Under the ripples," Abram said, "the tide is all one thing." Still he did not look up. Bita realized he wasn't going to until after they left.

"God is the tide," she said.

"You have a short time," he said. "The seers of Israel will tell you that much."

Arturus was looking at the shadows cast by the priest's body on the floor behind him. It made him think of something huge with wings, a dark angel with a long face, the reddish light like a dim sea of fire. He let his imagination picture Hell and then himself dressed as David, armed with sling and staff, confronting the giant devil-shape. . . .

"Come, my son," Bita said, and they stood quietly.

Abram didn't move or look up. "Farewell, my father," she told him. He nodded and began chanting, softly, under his breath and said no more to them.

Sunset. The small clay-brick and wooden buildings were cemented together by the deepening shadows as the last ruby-blood sun-stains thickened in the west.

Up the street slope Jerusalem's chief temple was a round silhouette. Meat was frying in fat somewhere nearby, and the greasy smoke stung Leitus' eyes as he and Ben Ymir followed the dirt street past a tethered row of kneeling camels that jerked restless heads and grunted disgruntled gutturals.

"I am uneasy," said the Jew, not looking at his companion.

"I feel delightful," Leitus reacted. He stared straight ahead, worrying about his son. He was sick of an outcast's life, of continual danger and the conspiracy to survive. They'd had a little breathing space among the Jews, although he never completely understood why they'd accepted them, in a harsh and pressing world.

He kept thinking about Arturus as they moved quietly through the twisting, crowded lanes. Remembered the first time infant hands circled his thumb and when the trusting eyes of the precious little tyrant, who ruled him with gurgles and wails, first seemed to focus on his face. He sighed. Those things bound a man for life. A woman, he realized, didn't need them to be bound.

The nightmare of fifteen years ago had faded. The strange battles in the dark catacombs; the madness; the murders and violence that had led him to hang on a cross and drop halfway into death's pit—all that had faded. What had seemed magic, he'd concluded long ago, must have been fever.

"I fear, my friend," Arim Ben Ymir was saying, "that we cannot escape an ill fate." One stubby hand knotted and unknotted the hem of his robe's sleeve. "Besides," he went on, "I suffer from various discomforts, to begin with. More than are natural to a pious man."

"Discomforts." Leitus smiled slightly as they stepped over a puddle of offal. A big woman leaned from a doorway, calling a boy's name into the twilight streets. They were close to the temple now. "You mean your tooth pain, Ben Ymir?"

"Tooth? It should be only that!" The stocky man shook his head grimly. One arm made stiff gestures before his face. "The holy organs of my manhood are cursed by God. I am as Job himself."

"What's this?" asked Leitus, brightening somewhat. "What holy organs? Your balls, you mean?"

"Quite so, quite so, my friend. Ah, you chortle. You should only have the swelling and burning there that I have. No smile would cross your face." The little man sighed. "No smile at all. Hold your own over a hot fire and maybe you'd have a taste of how I feel."

Leitus was having trouble containing himself.

"You mean," he pressed, "you burned your balls?"

"No, no, you ass. The pain is like unto fire."

"Ah, I see."

"No, you do not."

They went on. The dome filled most of the sky now.

"You always have some ailment or affliction," Leitus said. "I lay it to your diet. Most troubles start in the belly."

"Ha, ha." Arim Ben Ymir gestured with scornful hands. "What did I feed my balls, then, Roman fool?" He jerked his head around to peer into the gathering darkness.

"You fear the shadows, Ben Ymir?"

"So would you, Roman, had you sense enough."

"I dread the solid Roman steel," said Leitus seriously. "That gives me pause."

Ben Ymir nodded.

"Yet the day will come when the Lord God will smite them sore," he said.

"I hope it's tomorrow."

Ben Ymir dipped into the mists of his scriptural memory. He was a camel driver and guide, not a student.

"Think on the fate of Ramses," he said, "whom Moses the Great saw shattered by God's hand."

"I missed that," said Leitus.

"Arr," grunted Ben Ymir, waving his arm in disgust.

Leitus paused suddenly and stared down the space between two buildings, where he thought something had moved. A bearded, bony man with a lantern on a thin chain came out of the alley, a bundle of what might have been hides slung over one shoulder.

Ben Ymir reset his hood with pudgy fingers. They went on.

"We'll have to leave the city," Leitus said.

"Umm. I suppose so."

"You needn't leave."

"You don't want me to point the way?"

"Of course. But I cannot ask you."

"I don't do it for you. I do it for your wife. And boy. Why should they suffer from your ignorance of the desert?"

Leitus smiled.

"Thank you, Arim Ben Ymir," he said. "Perhaps we'll find a cure for your swollen balls somewhere."

"Oh, I'm glad it amuses you. I burn with pain and you delight me with cruel talk." They'd reached the temple's outer wall. "Now hear me: I have an uncle, a seller of goods."

"How remarkable."

"In Bethlehem." He shrugged. "Not my favorite town. I like the real city. There's always some excitement."

"I have an uncle myself. He lives under a rock in the bay of Naples. Milles the mussel, they call him."

"What?"

They passed more camels tethered for the night. Two women were unrolling a rug in the rosy light of a doorway facing the temple. Smells of spice. A baby crying faintly down a courtyard.

"We could seek shelter with my uncle," Ben Ymir said.

Leitus was preoccupied with the idea that he was actually going to have to leave. Fate was forcing his life again. He was afraid, because he saw no purpose in it. To him, now, life was random dooms, like falling rocks on a mountain slope.

"Do what with whom?" he asked.

"My uncle. I just explained." The little man shook his head with disgust. Each step jolted a short, sharp sliver of pain in his testicles. "He's no holy saint and likes to rub garlic in his ears to keep the worms out of his brains, but, well, family is family."

"Garlic in his ears?"

"It's written in scripture."

"I missed that too." Leitus turned around. He felt something again. Something moved again. They stopped. Ben Ymir took advantage to relieve himself against the secular wall. "Someone's following."

Ben Ymir crouched and squinted into the darkness that squeezed the glow of scattered lamps to tiny, dull spots in night's hollowness.

"I see nothing," he said. His voice was tense and dry.

Leitus' heart was pounding; the shadow shape had been too big and moved more like a man than a camel. He rubbed his eyes and told himself he was just very tired. He'd been sleeping badly all week, had had too many dreams and a burning sensation in his bowels.

"Let's go on," he said.

A few yards on they came to the low-roofed straw and clay building abutting on the temple wall. They ducked in through the low door. They'd been living here for over a year. Inside it smelled of smoke and oil and herbs.

A single lamp fluttered its tiny flame on the table in the adjoining room. No other light. They stopped in the doorway. A man in rich, pale robes was kneeling along there. Ben Ymir bowed with startled respect.

"Rabbi," he said. "Why do you pray in here?"

The high priest didn't move. His face was actually pressed to the floor. Leitus stepped close and stooped over him.

"He's not praying in here," Leitus said. The man's

features were flattened into the packed dirt. Blood drooled from his parted mouth.

"God's mercy," whispered Ben Ymir. "He is dead?"

"The side of his head is crushed in."

"Murder."

"Unless he bowed hard enough to break his skull." Leitus stood up. "But where's my wife and son?"

"Who would murder a high priest of Israel? Why was he here?"

She was always involved with priests, Leitus thought. But he was surprised that a man of this rank would have been in his house.

He twisted to his feet because someone had followed noiselessly and was filling the doorway. The man must have been close to seven feet, he realized. Ben Ymir stepped backward in shock. The man wore a kind of turban and his face was covered like a dead man's or a tribesman's in a sandstorm. There had to be a tiny strip, reasoned Leitus, open where his eyes were.

The giant's hands hung open at his sides. A dagger nearly as long as a Roman sword was thrust through his belt.

"A leper," muttered Ben Ymir.

That's right, thought Leitus. *They wrap themselves like that. Yet by law he may not remain in the city.*

"Where is the woman and the boy?" the muffled, straining voice said, as if, thought Leitus, his throat were clogged by stones.

"Who are you to ask?" demanded the Roman. "How dare you come in my house?" His heart was beating too fast, and fear filled his stomach with a kind of dread the circumstances didn't quite explain—the feeling men have when confronting the uncanny.

"He knew not either," said the giant, motioning to the slain priest.

"Polluted one," said Ben Ymir, "your fate is already stoning. Yet you brag of slaying God's holy priest?" The small man's thick staff was raised. Outrage flooded him.

The leper wheezed a sound that might have been pain

or laughter or the last rattles of draining life.

Leitus went to the hearth and tugged loose a stone. The giant leper shuffled into the room, his body tilting as if one leg were longer than the other.

"Who sent you here?" Leitus demanded, exposing half his back as he pulled a handle, then a long blade from the crevice. He turned, holding it still in the scabbard.

"The Messiah Ben Haman," the straining voice ground at them. The long arms went out to grapple Ben Ymir, who struck a surprisingly hard and quick blow with his stick, which smashed into the giant's crotch. The rattling sound that was (thought Leitus) the laughter of hell sounded again.

"What sought you to strike, Jewish filth?" the leper asked. "Things long sloughed off by the holy?"

"Holy? Holy?" Arim Ben Ymir was beside himself. "You abomination of God! You—" One shockingly long arm angled and caught his throat like a viper stroke and lifted him effortlessly to his toe-tips. He dropped his staff.

Leitus still couldn't find the slit the giant had to be looking through. He circled closer, drawing the long barbarian blade he'd brought from under the earth.

We'll find what he sees with, he told himself.

Ben Ymir snatched his own dagger with one hand, even as he strangled, and tossed it straight into the monster's chest, where it stuck deep. And accomplished nothing.

"Next," rasped the voice at Leitus as the Jew thrashed, face swollen, blood trickling out of his mouth from the force of the long, gripping cloth-wrapped fingers, "next you will tell me where the witch and the boy are to be found."

Leitus had sweated in the arena to learn to kill, fought in Caesar's expeditionary army to win Britain, and had been trained by a wizard (though he recalled little of it and took that little for part of a long, feverish sickness) to strike with almost supernatural skill and speed. When he struck in anger it was almost as if an outside force amplified his skill. But most masters of anything, he'd come to learn, conceded as much.

Leitus stabbed for the masked eyes. It felt like thrusting into dry straw. The thing flung Ben Ymir aside, shrieking through that choked throat, and reeled wildly back through the door, all lurching angles and flapping cloths.

Leitus bent over Ben Ymir, who was drawing painful breaths.

"Can you rise?" he asked.

The little Jew gasped and nodded. His eyes were wild. "Ahh," he groaned.

"I have to find my family."

Ben Ymir made it to one knee, wobbling. He licked the blood from his lips.

"I saw it," he said. "That was the angel. . . . I saw it. . . ."

Leitus helped him up, and after a moment they went outside together into the night. There was no sign of the giant leper, if that was truly what it had been. Ben Ymir had a different opinion.

"Can you walk?" Leitus asked.

"Yes, my friend . . . but they are doomed. . . . We are doomed. . . . I saw—"

"Saw what?"

"That was the angel who comes . . . the angel of the dark."

"He was a mad, deformed leper."

Leitus looked up and down the streets. The stars were an intense, sugary brightness. He was working at calming himself to think where his wife and son would have gone. Then he realized he'd have to find Ahab Ben Judah, the young priest who often discussed abstruse, and, to Leitus, deluded, points of religion with his wife. He'd felt vaguely jealous more than once, so his looking for them with Judah did not necessarily mean he hoped to find them together.

"Come on," he said.

"He was emptiness," Ben Ymir was saying. "I saw into the pit without bottom. I saw through the angel as I hung there. I saw—"

"You were hurt and shocked," Leitus assured him as they headed around to the front of the temple. "I rid us of him."

"Yes? Where is he, then? Is he fallen?" Ben Ymir shook his head, huddling into himself. "No, no," he said, "and with my dagger in him too."

"He was unduly strong and mad. With the strength of madness."

"The strength of hell, my friend. Only the holy blade drove him away."

Leitus grinned as they went in the front arch, holding the scabbarded weapon over his shoulder.

"Oh, yes," he said. "I forgot about that."

But he was uneasy and he knew it. The dread had a sickly cold grip on his insides. He wanted to find his family and breathe again.

"Scoff not, unbeliever," said the Jew. "I saw—I saw—"

They found Ahab Ben Judah reading in the chamber of scrolls. A candelabrum lit his table. His beard was thin and strung over his chin.

He looked up. His eyes were large and remote. An old man dozed on the outskirts of the rosy light, white beard on his chest, slumped to the side in his chair like an infant.

"Ah," he said, "Leitus. You did well to come here."

"I hoped," Leitus said.

Arim Ben Ymir stood there rubbing his face, lost in his terrors. He tried not to look at the shadows at the edges of the flamelight. He was afraid he'd see things there, shapes and outlines. His mind had been shocked by black hollowness, as if those clawed hands had dangled him over the bottomless pit itself and showed him what waited. So he was mad. It would not always show, but the madness was forever there. A stain that a thousand bright days and peaceful sleeps would never entirely wash out.

"Rabbi," he muttered, "all your wisdom . . ."

"Yes?" inquired Ahab.

"Where are they, then?" demanded Leitus, holding himself just exactly where he could stay calm, holding himself with terrific care.

Ahab understood.

"They fled the city. I will tell you the way. Your wife said to tell you to follow and bring the sword. She said you would understand."

Ben Ymir guffawed.

"The sword," he said. "Yes. And wisdom. Bring it too. The Devil waits to eat it."

Ahab studied the stocky man.

"Is he drunk?" he asked.

"We had a close call," Leitus said.

"So did your wife and son."

"So I feared."

"But they left safely."

Ben Ymir chuckled and shook his head.

Ai, he sounded to himself. *Ai.* He kept his eyes from straying to the shadow edges that hinted things. "And where is safety? Tell me, wise ones? Anyplace where night can fall, his demons wait to eat you."

"A heart filled with God's light," said the young scholar, "knows no place of darkness."

Arim Ben Ymir sniggered. He almost looked at the shadows for spite. Just to draw the horrors into the room and show these fools.

"Hear me, Rabbi," he said, "you talk with the tongue. When they come for you, see then if you can hold back hell with words."

Before Ahab could respond, Leitus cut across the conversation:

"Give me directions. I have no time."

"How true," said Ben Ymir. "None do."

Leitus ignored him.

"Tell me, Priest," he demanded, just on the edge of

losing his calm. The old man stirred slightly and sighed in his doze.

Ahab Ben Judah was nodding, standing up, coming around toward the doorway that framed the young Roman against the darkness outside.

"Yes," he said. "Of course. Ride through the Olive Gate, then meet the way that leads past the place of the skull."

Leitus was already turning, moving outside just ahead of the panic that waited, hovered, at his back. He didn't look back to see if Ben Ymir was coming. He just managed not to run.

ANTONY

At the near bank of the Nile he paused to rest. He tethered the lathered horse to the nearest palm tree and sat with his back resting on the trunk, looking over the glimmering water into the molten line of sunset. The air was sweetly scented.

He wanted to sleep. Thought about it, because he wasn't actually tired. It was as if something soft and secret in the twilight were lulling him, soothing his frayed consciousness with dreamy promises of far, sweet places.

It had something to do, he believed, with what had happened to him under the pyramid. That strange, bodiless state, afloat in a tide of wondrous, incomprehensibly significant images. He believed he shouldn't be resting yet. That there was some obscure threat brooding over him in the mild and peaceful evening.

I'll have to find a boatman, he thought. *But it won't be easy at night. I'm better off not thinking, because if I think too much, I'll go mad.*

"I'll just shut my eyes for a moment," he murmured.

He couldn't be sure if he was asleep. He could see everything in what seemed an overbright moonglow. The landscape was deathly still. The river looked flat and slick as ice. The stars were blurred together as if seen through beads of water. His vision seemed wider than normal and took in what was behind him, if he wished.

And then something moved on the far shore. Something dark and large. An impression of wings and hardness. He sensed it was aware of him but couldn't see him clearly yet. Sensed stone-hard eyes trying to focus on him.

He shrank back into himself, afraid of that darkly glittering sight. Felt it was cold. Deadly cold.

He strained, shuddered, shivered, and was awake in the moonbright. The water was a hush of perfect silver.

He still believed, or half believed, he felt it out there in the far darkness. He stood up, heart racing a little. He backed up a few steps to the top of a dune slope. Paused and caught his breath.

He had to hurry. To Judea. The goddess (or fever madness—he wasn't sure) had told him so. He tried to remember more about that. When he shut his eyes, there was something like a map in his memory, a high view of the land, a glowing line stretched straight from the pyramid, showing him the way; and something that was not quite a voice told him to follow the path of Israel. And he understood that that was the way the Jews had fled from Egypt out of bondage. He knew the story.

There's little doubt I've gone mad, he thought, *but as that is the case, one way is as good as another.*

He opened his eyes. The faint thread had faded away. But that didn't matter because he knew he'd never stray from his insane direction. Fate would pull him along. Once you accepted it, he reasoned, it wasn't so bad.

He started moving, not looking left or right; he didn't want to have to see whatever might be lurking in the shadows.

He kicked the horse downriver, the sand *schluss*ing under the steady hooves. He headed for where the thin glowing line had intersected the shallow curve of the Nile.

The world has shrunk down too narrow for poor Antony to turn around in, he thought.

"Yes," he said aloud, into the soft rush of the cool, water-scented air. "Following myself I sped to disaster, so why not follow voices and visions?"

Because he'd almost had it. Almost an empire. Almost.

BRITAIN

"We routed the great enemy the year of your birth, Morga," the long-faced, blind, one-armed priest, Cavul, told her, lurching to the right and twisting back, painfully, straight again as they followed the forest trail between the dense pines, massive, sweet-smelling shadows barely shaped by ghostly moontinting.

She stepped quietly, seeming lost in inner depths, her face placid and lovely, a warning only in the sharp edge of her nose.

"You took my childhood from me," she said.

"No. We gave you greatness."

"What is that to a child?"

"It wasn't for the child that it was given."

"What is it to me now? Less than nothing. I do what I do because there's nothing else."

"You have not yet come into your inheritance." He smiled, lurching beside her, leaning on the too-long staff. "When you do you will know the joy of your powers and of he who loves you."

The forest was very still. Pale, slow gusts of mist unfolded down the slope.

"Someday," she said, almost without inflection.

"Yes," Cavul said. "Soon."

"Cold comfort."

"The truth."

They waded through the low streamers that blurred across the path like weightless surf.

Cavul pivoted on his staff, twisting his face to hers as if the blasted, lurid eyes could actually see.

"The truth is," she was saying, "you want me to slay my brother."

"Who told you this?" He was coldly furious.

"Not who. How? you should ask."

"Ah. The power stirs in you."

"Why should I kill my brother? I never met my brother."

"Half brother." He twisted partly around his staff, then managed another lurching step. "Because the remnants of the enemy will rally around him." He slammed the staff-end into the loamy earth. "The other, the unborn one, we cannot touch." His face tensed. A tic sprang in a web from one side of his mouth. "But *he* will come without a sword and will pass like a dream into mortal memories. We must shatter the sword while we can, else someday it will smite our necks. You will go and find your brother."

They crossed a gently rounded ridge where the dark trees opened into a steep, smooth valley slope. The mist gleamed like pools and runs of water down to the bottom forest darkness. They paused there.

"If I had anywhere else to go," she told him, "I would go there."

He tilted his head again as if to watch her. In his mind there were shadows, forms that fluttered and stirred in a vast dimness where deep red pools and rivers of what might have been muted fire pulsed, where slow billows of smoke spilled over vague, vast outlines suggesting gigantic carven structures whose black bones were underground mountains. . . .

"You," he whispered, "are the princess of the kingdom." She didn't react. The fogs unwound in the stillness. "Of the power," he finished.

JERUSALEM

Ahab Ben Judah was kneeling in the holy of holies, his face close to, but not touching, the sacred ark. He felt a pressure almost like static electricity subtly touching his bared face. His slender, almost translucent, yet dusky hands were clasped as he rocked slightly.

The old priest who'd been sleeping in the reading room knelt beside him, screened from the rest of the chamber by thick, fine hangings that enclosed the holy of holies.

"Thou hast cast them out, O Lord," he said, "into the desert places where the sun will sear their flesh and the wild beasts will rend them. Yet, if Thou willst, they shall find Thy secret places, yea, even Thy habitation."

The old man covered his face with his garment. When he spoke his voice was muffled.

"You sent them," he said.

"If," said Ahab, "they are who they are, no harm will befall them or their burden." He sighed and leaned back on his heels for a moment, unclasping his fine hands. "In any case, we could not have protected them for very much longer. The rebellion will fail. The Messiah Ben Joseph is not yet come."

"And if the *dybhks,* the devils, overcome them, then what becomes of us?" The muffling hood stirred as he spoke.

Ahab Ben Judah shrugged.

"Who has forged a sword to wound the spirit?" he asked. "What matter who fights today? The Romans will slay our people, yet the mouth of time will swallow them too." His eyes shut. "Yet Israel will still exist, yes, even to the end of time." He felt the inexplicable energy of the Ark of the Covenant pressing at him, seeming to move the stray ringlets of his oily hair. "Israel will lie smashed and broken on the harsh stones of history, yet will never die." He trembled now with the pent-up force within him, with strange joy and terror mixed. "Israel is in the heart, not of a single nation or a single man, but in all hearts, and what wells from the heart lives from everlasting to everlasting!"

"Aiii," intoned the old man under his muffling cloth. "Yet again, why do we struggle since nothing can be won?"

"It is our nature," replied Ahab.

Bita and her son passed through the city gate about sunset. Their camels followed the road through the rocky, partly barren hills beyond the city. The sun was setting like a smear of burning blood behind the slope where the Romans executed prisoners. The crosses cast long shadows down the bare hill.

When Leitus passed later, at night, with Ben Ymir, the moon showed Golgotha in dark silhouette and he remembered—as on any damp day when his hands would feel where the nails had been driven through. There were fat and dark scars like corroded coins clutched in his palms.

He worked at never thinking too much about that time. He'd been sick with pain and fever, so what seemed to happen later—the battling in underground corridors with nightmarish creatures, falling through furnace skies into impossible landscapes—had all been his sickness. . . .

Arturus stared at the suffering and dead suspended above the grim hill in the blood-colored light that seemed to flood down over the shadowed rocks.

He thought something had moved along the slope. Something humped and large. His heart thumped once and his skin prickled. Something he couldn't recognize looked like it flowed downslope toward them. Or, he wondered, was he seeing dreams, as when he would sit with the priests and his mother, so still that he couldn't tell events of sleep from waking?

"Mother," he said as the camel swayed into a ravine where the road was all hard, smooth stones, so that the big hooves clacked and scraped.

"Yes?"

"I thought I just saw something strange."

"Put it from your mind," she said intensely. "Think about nothing."

That night, passing the same place, Ben Ymir said:

"See how the Romans butcher us."

"They butcher everyone," Leitus said, not looking at the moon-shadowed hill. "Themselves as well."

The hooves clacked like cracked stones.

"I don't like this place," said Ben Ymir.

"Yes."

"I feel somebody's . . ."

"Yes?"

"Watching." He shrugged and gestured meaninglessly, resitting his saddle.

"I doubt it," said Leitus. Because he was sure they (whoever they were) were at his wife and son's heels. More fanatics who believed in strange powers and unseen armies battling for control of man's fate. He knew they would want the sword he carried too. He kept it because of its value and the fact that it had never failed him, and because the jewels he'd pried from the hilt had succored them ten times over. "But we'll all soon meet, I think." *If I get them away this time, we'll go north. To Britain, perhaps. Why not?*

They kept a quick pace through the night. There was enough moon.

• • •

Bita and her son followed the high-walled ravine that had ceased to be a road several miles back. She realized she'd turned wrong in the darkness. They were following a dry watercourse now, pebbles grinding under the uneven strides of the camels.

Arturus kept glancing back, twisting in the saddle, to see if they were being followed.

"Where will your family lead us?" Arim Ben Ymir asked Leitus as they followed the roadway.

Leitus winced.

"Gizah," he said.

"What? In Egypt?"

"Unless they moved it."

"Ai. Why?" He shifted in the saddle and the next bump took him wrong. "Aii!" he cried. His hand went between his legs to shift things. "God's curse! God's curse!"

Leitus glanced back. He could just distinguish the other rider behind him in the moonwash.

"The demons have you again?" he wondered.

"The pain of Gehenna . . . ai . . . seizes me. . . ." He slammed the camel's neck. "Cursed beast!"

"The camel now?"

"My poor parts . . . ai . . ."

Leitus smiled, understood, and paid scant attention as Ben Ymir went on grumbling and sighing over his miseries. Leitus was thinking about his wife and her idea that only the holiness within would deliver them all in the end.

Splendid ideas, he thought.

Ben Ymir gritted his teeth and felt the pain decrease by frustrating increments. And his back tooth hurt again. He sighed. That was all he needed. But at least it took his mind away from the black visions that he believed hovered, shapeless, at the periphery of his sight. He believed he'd be fine so long as he didn't actually turn his head to look straight at whatever it was.

He was thinking how he'd chosen a senseless line of work. He should have been a market man or opened a shop. It was a young man's folly, he reasoned, to choose the outdoor life and meaningless freedom to roam. He had no wife or prospects of one. Nothing (or very little) put aside. A body that was betraying him, piece by piece. He was forty-five years old, and there he was, wandering among the heathen with Romans on one side and killers from hell on the other.

"I chose wrongly," he muttered.

"What?" Leitus wondered, abstracted himself.

Holiness within, Ben Ymir thought.

In the ravine, moving at a twisted angle to the highway her husband and his companion were on, Bita was concentrating as her mount swayed and crunched over the gravelly wash. She was trying, for the first time in many years, to reawaken the talent that had nearly destroyed her in Rome. She was trying to see through time and space again. She knew the risk: deadly beings that Leitus insisted were imaginary would feel her presence and try to find her and the boy. Ahab Ben Judah had warned her to stay dormant and wait, as he put it, for God to shake her by the shoulder. But her need was keen. They were lost, and deadly things were already on their trail if not on their heels. Ahab knew that, she considered. He was wise, but he'd never had to face what she'd faced in the depths of earth's darkness and terror. The sword could be lost, and worse. Because she never forgot the prophecy that her son would be taken from her this year, and she refused to accept it. She had never even mentioned it to Ahab or Abram for fear of their opinions. Her husband, she knew, had never really believed it. He'd protected himself, she felt, by saying no to all the terrible things that had happened to them. She understood. But she had no such release. And she knew or sensed that his test would be terrible. Better not to know too much. Arturus already knew too much. Knowing too much had eaten up his boyhood.

So she concentrated in the moon-splashed darkness and asked for the veil to rip between the worlds again. Rolled with the swaying humps she sat between and called to the golden beings from the higher worlds and overrode her fear that the dark ones below would hear her cry. . . .

But my wife has passion and speaks well, Leitus was thinking at that same moment. *She's magnificent, in her way, and I still love her and bless the day I was man enough to admit as much.* It haunted him, sometimes, that he'd nearly let her go more than once. What had she said one night as they were crossing the waste places to find Jerusalem, years ago? It came back to him suddenly and he felt warm with loving her. "Holiness whispers in the sand and kisses the air with the tenderness of a babe. It speaks when the sun is rising and sighs among the pure stars of heaven." He'd seen tears on her cheeks in the moonlight as he looked back at her sitting on the mule, the child asleep in her lap.

Leitus blew out his breath, straining to see ahead where the road bent across the rugged country, hoping to see them, hoping they'd stopped on the shoulder to rest, strained into the silver-shadowed night. . . .

She'd realized a little while ago that the sides of the zig-zagging ravine were gradually rising as they went on, coming closer together. She was afraid they were riding into a dead end.

She sat as still as possible and tried to rend the veil. Letting the camel find its own way, she shut her eyes in total concentration. It was a poor time to be trying it, she knew, but she was desperate to see something ahead.

Arturus was speaking, but she didn't really hear. There was something; the darkness shook like a loose cloth in a wind gust. A blurred glimpse of the rocky hills and sweep of desert ahead and the briefest flash of tall, thin, pale figures not far behind them, figures that stood out from night's blotting like red-hot, glowing stone. Just a flash and then she was panting, dizzy in the saddle, clinging to the big, dipping neck as they twisted through the narrowing defile.

"Mother," Arturus was saying. "What's wrong?"

"I'm all right," she said, recovering herself. "Don't be alarmed. We'll soon be out of here."

"Are you sure? I think we're lost."

"No. The desert is just ahead."

She hoped. She hadn't been sure in that brief flickering view whether this cut went all the way out. The water might run underground somewhere ahead, in the season when water ran out there. The idea of going underground with those nameless shapes at her back was grim. She made up her mind that they'd climb the sides first. Those things, she believed, came from under the earth and would have terrible powers in their natural surroundings.

"Will the camels fit?" the boy asked.

"Fit where?"

"If this gets narrower. I can touch the walls now." He stretched his arms out and could just scrape both sides.

"Then we'll walk, son," she told him.

"We should have gone to Bethlehem," Ben Ymir said to Leitus as they reached the edge of the desert country. There were long, flat stretches ahead that could have been lakes in the moonlight. "Despite my uncle dwelling there, some say it is a place of great holiness."

"Holiness," said Leitus, exasperated. "Ah, yes. Holiness. My wife is fond of talking about that." He shook his head. "I like to think about bronze and steel, squalor, disease, and all manner of suffering, myself."

"Ai, I don't have to think about these things," agreed Ben Ymir, "all save bronze and steel."

"And madness and untimely death."

"Few ever find it timely," philosophized the Jew.

Leitus had come to believe that they were all dreaming, tortured lumps of briefly and inexplicably animate meat who, somehow, had moments of tenderness and flickers of wisdom.

"Gladiators know the truth," he said.

Ben Ymir was trying not to look at the shadows in his mind. His words were automatic.

"He will comfort us," he intoned, "in the hour of our despair."

"Tsst," sneered Leitus. "Will he, now?"

"I have faith," insisted Ben Ymir, not quite desperately.

"I envy you," muttered Leitus.

The camels' sides were just about scraping the walls when the ravine ended. Bita and Arturus were suddenly in desert country: dark rock ridges and the beginning of the dunes.

The sudden open space was like a shock to them. Vast sky crusted with stars. The moon was bright enough to blink at.

Her son moved his mount up beside her. They swayed along together.

"Which way, Mother?" he asked. He was thinking about the others his own age in the temple school. He shrugged. He really didn't know any of them very well. There was never much time for play or casual talk. On the other hand, Deborah, the softly rounded, dark-eyed daughter of the wine-seller in their street, kept coming to mind. He often thought about her at night, just before sleep took him. The wind had once blown out her robe and he'd seen the flash of her strong, full-shaped, sleek legs as she'd stepped over a puddle, crossing the empty lot beside her father's shop. He liked to picture those legs and sometimes he'd hug the bedclothes, imagine kissing her while his body half-consciously stroked itself rhythmically against a lump in the blanket.

"We follow the moon to where it sets," she said. And then stopped because she saw it: a dark mass of armed men, moon glinting on armor and shield, moving out of the desert almost directly at them. As if they'd come to a rendezvous. And there was no going back.

"Do we run, Mother?"

The ragged foothills they'd just emerged from stretched right and left at their backs. The camels would get nowhere trying to break away. And who knew how many more troops there were out there? She didn't. Her flash of vision, if it had been actual had been spotty at best.

"No," she said, concentrating within herself, starting to gather the power that she hadn't used since he was born but which she knew was still there like a pool in a deep well. "I have a few tricks left," she assured him.

"Do we fight?" Because that was something he knew about. Any young man trained to a fine edge can't help but want to see what he can actually do. He felt alert, nervous, ready. He wasn't really conscious yet that these were fully armed and armored troops out there.

She smiled faintly.

"Do you think they're Herod's men?" she asked him.

"I can't tell."

"They're Romans, if I'm not mistaken."

They were. A hundred. A full century led by a centurion on horseback. The troops halted as the leader rode over to Bita and her son.

MORGA

The long, low, black, single-sailed ship ran quickly across the calm water through billows of low-lying mist. The half moon was overhead; the sky was perfectly clear. The big, square black sail creaked and thumped quietly. The bow waves hissed. The mist ripped soft and silent.

Morga stood on the aft platform deck, one icy white hand on the rail. The wind fluttered her black hooded robe. The blind priest Cavul balanced himself beside her, leaning on his staff. They overlooked two rows of oarsmen. The oars were shipped as the slim ship ran under sail alone. The rowers were tall, wrapped in black from head to foot.

A very tall priest in the same black hooded robes gripped the steering sweep.

"We are entering the river mouth," he called out.

"Good, good," said Cavul. "We near the land of secrets."

She stared at the mists that flowed steadily, luminously, past. She thought about why she'd agreed to come all the way from Britain to what she considered the ends of the earth.

"Do I steer straight upriver?"

"Yes, yes," said the chief priest, twisting partly around his staff, his blind, white-blasted eyes glaring ahead as if he actually saw. "We'll be told where to put in."

Told, she thought. *By my servants. At least so they say. . . . I have so many things I never asked for.* But she'd been told by what she called the voice in the pit that in the land of Egypt she would find the answers she craved to know: who was her actual father and what was really going to happen to her. She was sick of priests' allusions to her great destiny. *It's all stupid and cold and cruel and means nothing,* she thought. *They have no idea why anything is anything. No one ever can answer me. Sometimes I want to hurt things because only pain is real . . . that's what they don't want to face . . . only pain . . . the rest is just coldness.* Because she had seen young boys and girls playing and flirting, older ones meeting in the forest to touch each other and kiss, pressed close together. . . . It seemed terrifying to her in its meaninglessness. She could understand eating, drinking, sleeping, and looking around at sights that were interesting. She always was interested when things died, especially animals and people. She'd been about seven when she saw a quarry mule crushed by a stone and the driver with one arm splintered and shattered, and she'd thought: *I am made of the same mucky stuff.* And the dead men and women on the hill where crimes were punished (though why one senseless act was a crime and another won praise eluded her utterly—as it had older philosophers) fascinated her because it was clear they didn't matter. They'd simply stopped moving around. Everything would stop moving, in time. Very often she was anxious to stop moving herself. So why would those couples press together and seek one another out so particularly? She made nothing of it. And she didn't ask anyone, much less a priest, because no one ever really answered her questions. *I eat and sleep and look at things because I move around and can't help it because my insides move by themselves and some things taste better and are more interesting than others. But I see the dogs are the same and, for all I know, the worms. When my insides die I'll stop just like the dogs.* Except there was a strangeness in her, a wanting she couldn't explain any more than she knew what was wanted. And when it pressed her she'd think how they were all dull and senseless around her, all of them as dull as dogs, not understanding how they were lumps that moved and then stopped, and she'd want to hurt them, stop them, make them see there was nothing but the end, the cold emptiness, when it pressed her with strange wanting. . . . Normally there was just the coldness.

She was feeling it right then. Her hands were sweaty and she kept finding them balled into tight fists. Her fingers ached when she straightened them.

"Hurry," she said to no one in particular. "Make speed!"

Because she wanted the answers, needed them. Because the other urge was growing stronger and made her want to strike out, send her servants out into the night to rend and kill all the fools, show them what they were and that all must stop in total blackness in the end, that they were all senseless vapors. Now was one of the times she hoped their promises were true, that she would be queen of the world and have her will.

"Hurry," she whispered, hands clenched, pale and tight.

IN THE DESERT

Leitus heard hoofbeats. Knew they were horses and maybe half a mile behind, coming fast. That meant, if they were after them, they didn't expect a long desert chase.

"Ai," said Ben Ymir. "Just as I expected."

"What did you expect?" Leitus said, using the whisk, urging the animal on faster.

"Misery and doom." His mount kept pace with the other as they headed for the loosest sand, looking for dunes where the camels would have a major advantage.

"I don't think it's the devils after us," Leitus said. He kept glancing back across the open, moon-spattered country and thought he made out a vague line of riders crossing a low hill, flickering across the starry field behind.

"What matter," sighed Ben Ymir. "It comes to the same thing in the end." He saw that darkness again before he twisted his mind away from the image. The emptiness behind all things. The hollow horror that would eat all life, all hope. *Ai,* he thought.

Leitus was thinking about Bita and hoping he'd distracted the pursuit—except he knew better. The power of the State was behind it all, he was sure.

He felt suddenly very tender, thinking about her.

Let her believe whatever she likes, he said to himself, *so long as it brings her comfort . . . . May the gods or the one God, if she likes, keep her and bless my son.*

Except the words were dead in his mind. The sentiment was real, but he might as well have addressed it to a stone.

Now there was sand swooshing under the bony, awkward, powerful legs of his mount. The half moon was out in front of them, its illumination swallowed like pale water in the dune shadows. There was a sweet smell of wild herbs in the air. Leitus wondered vaguely where they grew out here.

"They still come," Ben Ymir called over the windrush and the camel grunts and the spray of sand. "Many riders, and they've seen us."

ANTONY

By the time he'd ridden a day and night across the desert country, the visions he'd had in the underground passageways had faded, and he felt a little like a man coming back to himself after a feverish sickness. He was still very thin, but he'd been gnawing dried meat and hard bread, drinking nearly all his water, and was stronger and felt more substantial.

And now he was starting to doubt his direction. But it was too late to turn back. He'd have to push straight on and hope for the best.

Within an hour he smelled water. The horse had already aimed for it, cutting against the loosely held reins. The moon was high now and he could see the clumped trees of an oasis.

"A sign from the gods," he muttered. He couldn't have gone back, he reflected, because the horse would have been dead by midday tomorrow in any direction but this one. He half believed it was a sign, and the feeble fabric of his confidence in the gleaming woman-shape that had wordlessly spoken to him was stitched a little tighter.

BITA

As the Romans closed in around them she tried to remember the last flickers of the vision. She'd reached out, but there'd been no trace of the golden light or the golden voices—just the shadows. She wondered, with the first stirring of a terrible fear, if the golden Avalonians who inhabited the core of the sun had been utterly defeated. If they had, the earth was doomed to darkness. Ahab Ben Judah had described the blast of black lightning hurled by dread Aataatana, lord of the underworld, the bolt that had streamed into the sun and rent the worlds of light with scars and cracks and spatters of dead darkness. She shuddered, imagining that glowing, sweet, subtle dimension shattered forever.

As the centurion rode up and stopped, she remembered talking to Abram, the high priest, remembered the somber depths of his dark and deep-set eyes. "The Seraphim and Cherubim are known to me," he'd said, as if reciting. "As are the ways of hell." "They spoke to me," she'd told him. "Do you believe that?" he'd asked. "I know it," she'd replied. "Then," he'd said, "their seal is set upon you, for those with eyes to see."

It had been afternoon. He'd stopped by the well where she'd been drawing water. He'd come right up to her, as if he'd known her, that first meeting, leaned on his staff, and asked where she'd come from. The conversation had reached the real point soon enough: "You are fighting the hidden war,'' he'd said, watching her with eyes like glazed dark stones. She'd shaken her head. ''No more,'' she'd replied. ''Heaven has been silent.'' ''No,'' he'd said, ''heaven is never silent. You have simply not been listening.'' The conversation had a dreamlike quality for her. ''You will fight again. But the sword matters, as you shall see, less than the jewel.'' She remembered all this now. And was still puzzled. ''What jewel, sir?'' she'd asked him. ''Perhaps it is not a jewel, then,'' he'd said. ''What, is it something else?'' she'd tried. ''Perhaps not,'' he'd said, and said no more on the subject then or ever again.

And now, she was thinking, *he has cast us loose to reach the shore or perish. Is this jewel the key? For Abram never jests or speaks things in vain. May the one God open my mind and soul to the light.*

The moon glittered on the mounted centurion's leather and brass chestplate and plumed helmet. The camels wheezed and squawked. The horse blew loose-lipped breath as the bulky man held it in place while the line of troops half-circled them.

The centurion's face was a shadow. His voice was husky, as if forming words were a physical strain.

''Hold where you are,'' he said.

''Will we have to fight, Mother?'' Arturus asked in Hebrew.

''Are there more of you coming?'' the Roman asked. He leaned thoughtfully in the saddle.

''No,'' she said. ''May we go on?''

That appeared to amuse him.

''You may go,'' he replied, ''but where you end may not please you, woman.''

She felt death there. Under everything. Behind everything. These men were like gears in a machine. She wondered who'd wound the spring.

I'll strike him down, she thought, *and tell Arturus to flee. He may have a chance that way.*

''Why slay us?'' she asked.

The man sat tilted with the quiet assurance of one hundred armed legionaries at his back and beck.

"Why not? You are Jews. All Jews are rebels who prowl the desert dark." His voice was a whispery strained sound in the night's hush. "We have orders to slay rebels." He shrugged.

One of us will be lost to these, she thought. *It had best be me.* Because the darkness knew and hated them and dreaded what the Jews promised and the prophets in the desert shrilled and the lonely winds echoed and the wheeling stars sketched in bright image on the skies: the golden light was coming back to this bleak, barren world. *Maybe that is the jewel,* she thought.

The darkness had turned the spring tight, had set the brassy gears grinding to crush them.

"And if," she tried, "we were Romans?"

"Then a less pleasant death," he told her, "reserved for traitors."

"And if I ask why are we traitors," she tried, "you'll tell me because we *seem* to be Jews."

He said nothing. The crunch, bump and muted clang of the soldiers closed them in now. The centurion raised his arm in an almost lazy gesture. When it arced down they'd die, by moonlight, to no purpose. And her boy would be lost.

He'll have to risk the ravine.

She prepared herself, gathered her inner force, to strike down the leader. She wondered how much of the old power she still had. No time to test.

Sharply, in Hebrew, she ordered her son to ride back into the narrow defile toward the other, perhaps worse, danger; but as the arm fell, as the swords came level in a dozen killer hands, the three followers (she'd not clearly counted) came out of the ravine's edge of pitch-black shadow.

She flexed and hurled her will against the centurion. She'd once stopped Marc Antony as if he'd struck a stone wall, but that was years ago. This blocky fighter only reeled slightly in the saddle.

"Ride, son!" she shouted.

His sword was out. His mouth was dry. His mother led the way straight at the narrow space between the nearest two soldiers. They hadn't dressed ranks tightly. Who would have, faced merely with a boy and a woman?

She struck invisibly at the Roman nearest her son. She had just enough power left to delay his thrust and dull his reflex cover-up so that Arturus' downstroke laid open the side of his face. She leaned away from the man in front of her. The camel screeched as the short sword raked its ribs, but she managed to get through the narrow space behind her son.

"We're free!" exulted the boy, waving his sword. His heart drummed in his ears, his blood wild with excitement.

"Don't slow your pace!" she yelled over the tumult at their backs. The men on their flanks were racing now to try and cut them off. Stones buzzed past their heads as slingmen let loose.

She took one look back: metal glinted in the moonbright; shadows tangled; the centurion yelled orders, trying to get his horse through the mass of his men; and then there were screams.

Who was screaming? she asked herself.

She couldn't tell. Several soldiers were throwing away their shields and weapons and running in panic. From what? And then one of the three thin, humpbacked, long-limbed giants who'd been following them, wrapped in flapping rags like lepers or the dead in winding sheets, appeared in the Roman ranks. Then another, too-long arms clawing with superhuman speed and strength, flinging the shields aside, ripping men to the sand, tossing them aside like stuffed toys.

"Ride hard, Arturus," she commanded. "Ride hard!"

LEITUS AND BEN YMIR

By dawn they were exausted. Ben Ymir clung to his camel's neck and half dozed. Leitus kept shaking himself awake. The sun rose behind them and stretched their shadows, immense and contorted. There were no pursuers visible on the horizon.

The Jew was complaining now and then, lips cracked and sore. He squinted into the sunrise.

"Like Job I toil through misery," he muttered. "Forsaken by God and men. Ai . . ."

"My heart weeps for you," said Leitus, staring across the rosy glow of endless dunes.

"And now, boils on my backside from wrong sitting. . . ."

"You're an expert man of the desert, I thought," said Leitus, closing one eye because he couldn't quite focus two at once. "And a camel ride distresses you?"

"Ai, yes, when a man must sit unnaturally to spare his balls and speed to stay a step ahead of doom."

"The devils seem to have lost our trail."

Ben Ymir swayed upright again and winced. There was no comfort. He sighed. A few flies buzzed around them, attracted by rank camel-stink and unwashed humans.

"The men did," Ben Ymir said. "The others never will."

"Where are we, O lodestone of the desert?" Leitus fumbled around for his waterskin, then wet his sore lips.

"Lost," said the Jew.

"I'm not surprised," Leitus said, savoring the few drops on his fuzzy tongue.

BITA

How fast can they run? she asked herself. They were well out into the desert now. The camels rolled on steadily. She kept the moon behind them as it rose.

"What happened, Mother? Are we safe?" He craned his neck to look back across the waves of sand. He felt relief and satisfaction, too, replaying the fight in his mind: the charge of the camels into the line, his blow, which had seemed feeble to him at the time, catching the trained Roman and knocking him aside. He wanted to do it again. He remembered being afraid, but that was nothing; the blow, the action, brushed the fear aside.

"For now," she told him.

"Do you think Father will find us out here?"

"I don't know. But he knows where we'll meet."

Arturus was dozing in the saddle hours later, the moon setting now in the clear, cool air. The sand slushed as the tireless, awkward beasts kept their pace across blank, silvered darkness.

Bita's eyes were remarkably sharp at night. She saw the trees a long way off. She tried to feel the enemy behind them, but didn't have the strength to try for more than that, to rend the veil again.

"We'll rest soon," she told him.

ANTONY

He bent over water, which was like a hole in the earth. His outline was a shadow on the reflection of clustered stars. When he cupped a mouthful, the image shattered. The drink was cool, muddy, and sweetish. The palm leaves made a soft rushing clatter in the breeze.

"I'm a coward," he murmured. *I didn't want to face her at the end.*

But he was going to, after all, and he knew it. He'd rest and eat and find his way to Alexandria. The underground vision, he tried to believe, was no doubt billowed out by his fear. The fear that chewed his soul. The fear that tensed his innards and left food stale in his mouth and a gripe in his belly; fear that took the savor from wine.

He sighed. Cupped more water and drank deep. Let himself slump and sag on the sand and grasses and moist dirt.

Sleep now, he thought.

And then he realized he wasn't alone. And next felt the unmistakable point between his shoulders.

"Contain yourself," he said. "I'm but a thirsty, weary man. You need not fear me. The time when I was fearful is past."

On the water surface the ripples settled, and the stars reformed from streaks and broken blurs.

SUBIUS MAGNUS

"I cannot believe it," Subius said to no one in particular. He squinted into the bright haze that dissolved the horizon around the bulky, wallowing merchant vessel. Bright blue, warm waves slap-slapped the hull in a soothing rhythm.

The seaman nearest him emptied a slop-bucket over the low rail. The man was small and burnt brown, and had long, stringy black hair in contrast to the massive, rounded, bald ex-gladiator.

The seaman watched, with some satisfaction, as the garbage bubbled and drifted along the hull.

Subius gently rubbed the sunburned crown of his head where the leathery tan was red-raw. His eyebrows were bleached to coppery glints across his heavy forehead. He pursed his surprisingly small, almost feminine mouth, thoughtfully.

"I still cannot believe it," he repeated.

The seaman set down the bucket and favored him with a skeptical look. Back amidships, three crewmen were checking the cargo lashings while another was wiping down the polished deck with a soft cloth.

Subius thumped the rail with both huge fists. The seaman just watched and waited. He was thinking how all owners were mad and bad luck aboard. They worried and had no real duties, were always underfoot and prone to pointless conversations.

I cannot believe she did it, Subius thought. *Not a word in all those years. Not a hint.* Thirteen years, more or less since he'd met Sira, a freewoman, widowed daughter of a dead tavernkeeper. She'd worked for her uncle, who'd taken over the business. Thirteen years ago, on his first trip to Egypt, he'd been looking for Leitus and Bita. He'd heard they'd gone to the eastern provinces. He'd found Sira instead. Spent some months with her. *I should have said yes and married her, but what did I know then? How could she not have told me?* And then he'd been back twice in later years, five years ago the last time, and she'd said nothing. She hadn't even come downstairs. Her uncle, backed by some oily wandering Mongol ex-wrestler, had done most of the talking. Her uncle was a short, wide-shouldered man with light eyes and a frosty smile. He had leaned in the doorway with the greasy one standing behind him carefully, curling one oiled and drooping mustache end. *I should have stayed the first time, but I wanted to make my fortune first and not have to go begging for work.* He liked to believe that. He'd told her that, too, standing in the dusty courtyard of the inn while two women beat a rug over a line, a camel driver squatted against the wall and ate flatbread, someone inside scraped a pot and the seethe and bustle of the city sounded all around, told her while aiming his talk past the uncle in the doorway, certain that she was listening at the second-floor window above and expecting her to cry: "Wait!" as he headed back out the whitestone arch into the chaos of the commercial street. He'd even paused and looked back, but all the windows were full of sharp, empty shadows, holes in the white brick.

"She never said I had a daughter," he said, in the general direction of the wiry seaman. The man didn't quite smirk. He'd have something to grin over later in the crew's quarters. "Incredible." Subius felt the malt brew he'd had with lunch squeezing his consciousness with numbing fingers. He liked the feeling, though he favored wine. He'd always favored wine.

"Ah," said the seaman.

"I should have stayed in Rome." Because he was afraid of it, too, and was just starting to face the fact.

"That's right, me lord," the seaman said.

"So you agree?" *They have to treat me with the same contemptuous respect I would have treated me with back in the days when I owned nothing but my bare life and was ever about to lose that. . . . Hah. And now I'm worried that maybe she will let me in the damned place this time.*

He turned and leaned his powerful hams into the woodwork.

"As you say, me lord," the man was saying.

"Don't like excess ballast on board, eh?" Subius asked, grinning slightly. "But think how useful I'd be if we meet with pirates, for instance."

"Ah, for ransom."

The ex-gladiator chuckled.

"Yes, my price comes high," he said. *All your blood and entrails.* No one on the ship knew he had ever been anything but a smooth-bodied merchant.

I should turn the ship and never set foot in Alexandria. . . .

Because he sensed the easy days were over again. The grim things he'd put partly from his mind. He'd been drunk through most of the worst days; he still drank when the weather went sour.

He'd found a handful of loot on various bodies on a night fifteen years before when he'd followed young Leitus, whose life he'd been charged to preserve by dying Spartacus, into the ogre Iro's underground hellhole, Leitus limping on swollen feet, hands broken and puffy where the nails had pinned him to the cross. He'd been very drunk and remembered only flashes and blurred sequences until the next morning, when he'd taken gold coins and jewels from the dead in a hangover haze. . . . He'd found his way out, wandered to the coast, and eventually bought a ship from a Persian tradesman (who needed a gambling debt satisfied) in the violent, exotic seaport city of Brindisium. . . . Eventually there were more ships and days on the coasts of Italy and the

East until the golden sun had baked the dark memories away. He'd had full-bodied mistresses in three cities at one point and worried about local politics and taxes, duties on cargo, gained soft flesh over his iron-hard underlay of muscles. Then he'd learned he had a daughter he'd never seen, in Egypt, and contentment had melted again. . . .

He frowned. Sighed.

They were half a day from landfall. He'd look and be a fool to turn back. He was of half a mind actually to give the order in private to the captain—the young captain, who looked, he thought, more like a bath boy in Rome than master of a vessel. But he knew his job, Subius had discovered. And he had such hopes and aspirations. Subius realized the fallacies, yet was won over by the purity of the fellow's expectations. Just having them meant more than any mere result, he'd decided, because the results were always torn and compromised. When Subius would rub him with sticky, gritty facts, the young captain would agree, nod, accept, and deplore, but always smiled quietly with serene confidence, as though to say: "Yes, yes, that's the bad course most things in life naturally run, but I simply won't allow it, in my own case. I simply won't, you understand."

I want to turn back. I'm too old for these things.

"Too old," he unconsciously voiced.

He turned back to the calm, lucent blue water and sky. Stared at the haze that shimmered before them like a whitish wall shrouding his future.

"Good afternoon, sir," said an energetic voice.

Subius didn't turn.

Just the one to encourage me, he thought dryly.

"Captain Weira," he said. The man was half Roman. He'd said, with a strange enthusiasm, that his father had been a German, as if that somehow gave him an advantage.

"Fine weather," the captain said.

"To turn around and run in," said Subius, staring at the haze.

"What's that, sir?"

"It's a fine day, I said. I might as well."

"We'll make landfall by sunset, as I reckon it." And Subius had the feeling he'd really reckoned it. He imagined him squinting seriously at whatever instruments and narrowly eyeing the sun. The captain loved the mechanics of sailing, the feeling of power over his fate. Subius was sure there was no wall of nothingness on Weira's horizon.

"You should have joined the navy," Subius told him.

"I like the merchant trade," was the earnest reply. "There's a future, you see. In the navy I'd wait ten years or more for a command."

"Yes," allowed Subius, finally turning. "Yet, bad luck or an owner's disfavor or pirates or politics could end your aspirations. How little in this life can be relied upon."

The youth nodded.

"I see that," he admitted, seeing nothing of the kind, his look fixed remotely on triumphs to come, adventures unfolding. "But if a man has a touch of fortune, and why not indeed, then a man might command a fleet in his time."

Subius sighed. "Never mind what I said," he told him. "You've filled me with hope and the promise of springtime." He twisted his mouth in a half-bitter smile.

"Sir?"

"Sir. I'm well respected now because I own ships."

The captain looked faintly injured. He blinked curling, dark lashes.

"I respect your judgment, sir," he told the massive man.

Subius chuckled.

"My judgment," he echoed. "May the gods help you, young captain, and not the judgment that has led me only from foolishness to folly." The young man looked puzzled. He obviously set great store by Subius, who could command respect by his mere presence most of the time. "I was a slave. A killer for the world's entertainment, and then, later, a killer for no one's." He twisted his delicate, incongruous mouth into wryness. "Never mind, never mind." Breathed deep. The air sparkled with rich life. "Sail on to your port of dreams, young captain." How sweet it would be to start again, fresh as a child.

The captain nodded seriously, as if he actually understood as much as the ex-gladiator was offering.

"Yes," the young man said.

"You'll prosper. The gods have assured me."

"Yes, I think I may at that, sir."

"Call me Subius," his master told him, turning back to stare again at the wall of vagueness that lay before them. "Once I set foot on that shore, there'll be no saving me."

"From what, sir . . . Subius?"

"From anything, young Captain. From anything."

CLEOPATRA

Her kidneys hurt. She could see the palace through the window slit in the small closet beside her main stateroom. Outside the water slip-slopped softly in furtive ripples along the hull of the royal barge. The oil lamps shone around the grounds and in the arched windows. But too few. The palace was half deserted.

She shifted her soft, bare buttocks on the golden seat over the jewel-encrusted tub. The little room was rich with silky hangings and scent and gleaming lamps of smokeless sweet oil.

One servant girl stood ready with a soft, wet, perfumed cloth.

The queen winced, strained, and shut her eyes against the cold stab of pain. So many had fled the city, she was thinking. The Romans were coming, virtually unopposed. Except they'd be fooled because Antony was bringing an army. There was no word of him because he was coming in secret. Yes, she was almost sure of that.

She opened her eyes but didn't look outside again.

"He'll return soon," she murmured.

They'll not drag me in chains through their damned city, she thought.

The dusky, smooth-featured girl said nothing. Her fear showed, though the queen paid no attention. The girl felt the world was ending and she would have run, except she had no idea where, since it was the whole world ending, with no spot or space to hide in. She lived in deep terror and thought her mistress brave beyond measure. The girl pictured doom rising like a wave over the sickly-pale city, a wash of darkness like a cloud shot here and there with the brassy, evil glimmer of Roman armor looming over them like the flame-drawn figures on the hangings of their chamber when the small flames shifted or sputtered.

"Not," the queen was saying aloud this time, "not where I was carried in triumph when great Caesar lived." She strained again. Her insides exuded a last, burning drop. "Ah," she whispered.

"Mistress?"

"Nothing, Sulti," Cleopatra said. "Wipe me now." She stood up, naked, thoughtful, the pain fading. The slave girl lightly dabbed the soft cloth between the golden tinted legs.

The polished copper mirror showed her a dim outline and she was glad of the lack of detail. She didn't want to see too much. Just tints and shapes to dream into, this near the end.

The price of softness, she thought, *is to wear away quickly. . . .*

She turned her head and stared through the window at the wan flames flickering in the empty window of the almost deserted city.

ROME

Trivian was uneasy. He kept giving himself good reasons for having come out here. He kept tapping his long fingers on the chariot side. The wheels ground along the unpaved road, the horses kept a steady pace, the driver and the other two senators leaned as they took a steep curve at moderate speed.

They were on the top of the hill, passing massive villas, tended lawns, lines of cypress trees like spikes. Dusk was blurring in, blending the suburb into a faintly violet, edgeless generality.

Rake-thin Senator Beto was saying to Trivian:

"This fat coward ought to wait on you. Why should you come out to him like this?"

"He wouldn't," Trivian said. He was an average-looking man, except for his eyes; they showed the hardness and calculation that accounted for his being Octavius Caesar's second-in-command. "And we need the son-of-a-bitch."

The summery evening air, scented by herbs, flowers, cooking, washed sweetly over them. The second senator, Nonverius, a short and nervous man, said:

"For what? His money? Must we ride to fawn on every rich bloat-belly in Rome?"

"Trust me," said Trivian, strangely without conviction. He realized he wasn't really sure why he'd agreed to come out to Flacchus' villa. He gave himself reasons, but none of them quite stood up.

Insects raved in the undergrowth. Fireflies drew golden streaks on the open lawns and fields. Oil lamps already shone softly in some windows.

Marc Antony used to live not so far from here, Trivian recalled. *A brave man, misguided to his doom by the cunt of a whore. . . .* But that was easy to say, he realized. And likely not true. Most men led themselves to their dooms by their own noses.

They were passing the low wall that enclosed the villa Flacchus had supposedly purchased from Iro Jacsa. No one had seen Iro in fifteen years to confirm or challenge the title. Many believed he'd been assassinated, but why would the already incredibly wealthy Flacchus have to kill a man for property? Unless there were some deeper reasons. Trivian wondered. No one had seen Flacchus for ten years either, and then, five years ago, he'd turned up in the Senate wearing old, stained robes and acting as if no time had passed since he had last taken his seat. He'd been presumed a casualty of the abortive slave rebellion led by the boy Leitus, who'd claimed to be the son of Spartacus.

Trivian was about to order the chariot to turn around and head back to the city. But, instead of giving the command, he drifted into a kind of reverie, recalling images from the past as the faintly violet twilight haze gradually deepened and shadows began to swallow the landscape.

Fat Flacchus, he was thinking, *just walking to his seat in those filthy rags. . . . He's a madman, for all his resources. . . . Were Octavian here, we'd soon strip him of his pretensions.*

Iro's villa had been boarded up and condemned as haunted by the priests. No one wanted to go there despite rumors of vast treasure in the catacombs supposed to honeycomb the hill under the main structure. A few youths had broken inside but found nothing and added to the tales of shadowy terrors lurking there and demon sounds under the earth.

They were just turning in the open gate.

"Turn back," Trivian thought he said.

"What, Senator?" asked the driver.

There were no guards or servants, just a line of statues on both sides of the drive. With no heads.

"We go back now," Trivian thought he repeated, louder.

They looked like statues of gods. The necks were shattered stone. Trivian noticed the heads were lying here and there on the lawn. He found it odd and disturbing. And why were they hauling to a halt before the villa steps?

"Are my orders without meaning?" he demanded.

The driver looked quizzical.

"Sir?" the man asked.

"Do I speak in vain?"

"What's wrong?" asked Beto.

Trivian blinked and rubbed his forehead. His head hurt. He hadn't noticed it before. That was odd too.

"Never mind," he muttered, "we're here."

The driver and the two others exchanged looks. The statues, pillars, and angles of the rambling villa gleamed the subtleties of twilight.

"It looks empty," commented the driver.

"Knock," said Nonverius to Beto, who was already on the steps.

But the iron-barred door scraped open and a small slave holding a lit taper limped out and stood waiting. His face was featureless, the candle flame just hinting the outline of his skull.

"Enter, sirs," he invited, his voice featureless too.

Inside the doorway no light showed. Trivian thought of a gate into nothingness. He thought: *Maybe the sound of the wheels and the horse feet drowned out my words. . . .*

He frowned and climbed down from the oversize chariot. Eased a crick in his back that the ride had aggravated. He was thinking about the rumors again, but they'd seen no portentous effects. No flicker of ghosts or demon wail. As they went inside he wondered which room had been the woman's, the sister's. The story was she'd been her brother's lover and that he'd murdered her and eaten part of her flesh, the liver or heart. Even the hardened watchmen had been horrified by the conditions of the bodies, so some said. This was all from fifteen years ago, of course, yet the stories had the currency of Caesar's murder.

They followed the crippled servant with the wan candle, feet twisted as he walked as if he meant to tiptoe. They followed him into a low-ceilinged room with red tapestries and paintings on the walls; there were enough tapers set in sconces to show up color here. The floor and ceiling seemed to be black marble.

An oppressive chamber, Trivian thought.

"Our host," said Beto.

The fat man was sitting (as if in the baths, Trivian said to himself) naked (no, there was a loincloth) on a low couch, body oiled or maybe sweaty, his belly resting on his legs. His oddly small and bony hands were neatly folded under his round chin.

He has the face of a nasty baby, thought Trivian.

"Noble senators," Flacchus greeted them, "good of you to attend me."

"What? Attend?" muttered Beto. "Is he become emperor?"

Flacchus smiled thinly. His stare seemed fixed on nothing.

"That is more or less why you are here," he told them.

"What's that?" Nonverius asked.

Trivian was puzzling over the fact that he hadn't offered them a seat. What was that fat bag of tricks playing at? He felt tense and decided to leave. Kept starting to say so and turn on his heel. Kept starting, but nothing seemed to happen. There was a dreamlike quality to all of this, he realized.

He was puzzling over it while Flacchus was saying:

"I could take time and gradually win you over to my way of thinking, but I suddenly find there is very little time left."

"Time?" Beto was expostulating. "Time for what? Nonsense by moonlight?"

"Be still, worm," hissed their flabby host.

"Worm?" responded Nonverius.

"You portly, stupid, miserable . . ." began Beto, but before the list of Flacchus' shortcomings could be extended, the fat man's small eyes glared flame red, almost like a cat's or dog's, and then a strange echo of fire seemed to flash in the skinny senator's pupils. He trembled and emitted a sighing moan.

"To your offal, worm," Flacchus said. He tittered. Because he was mounted on the power. He called the power and felt it respond, felt the hard outline of it under his big, soft buttocks. He scrunched himself around it, on its smooth, pulsing hardness. His tunic was opened under him and he wore no undergarments, so the smooth shape of power pressed between his flaccid hams and poured its dark strength up into his body against the normal grain, pushing up where foul things came out. "Down," he commanded, and Beto's legs sagged and he looked shocked and suddenly afraid. Tried to control his knees but ended staggering in a half circle on his haunches and then fell flat as if pressed down by an invisible hand. "Down," crowed the fat man. "Move as thou must!"

Beto lay flat on his belly and croaked in dismay, starting to wriggle across the smooth floor.

"What is this madness?" demanded Trivian.

Flacchus was chuckling, rocking back and forth. The dark power tingled, pouring up into him. He felt as though floating. He kicked his big, soft bare feet in a noiseless caper.

Nonverius studied the fat man's eyes, then silently bolted for the exit arch, vanishing into the shadows. Flacchus smiled gleefully and concentrated. Trivian heard a hideous splatting sound in the next room where the man had fled. It was like a burst melon. The livid flamelight seemed to melt and reform Flacchus' pale, soft features. The power filled him utterly. He was vast; his colorless sight reached beyond the chamber into the starry cavern of night and overlooked the world.

The power, he believed, was his alone. He'd sucked it, like a babe at the breast, at the bottom of ancient stone stairs that spiraled down the shaft to the rocky banks of the underground river that flowed from distant Britain, under this very building, which had been an old temple before Rome was even a dream. He'd fallen to the bottom of the stairs fifteen years ago and lain there holding the dark power stone that had kept him from actually dying. He'd shivered and twisted with fever for weeks while black visions opened dark secrets to him, and he came to know that the sphere he sat on, called the Black Grail by the druids, long before the Christians renamed the holy one a cup to honor their slaughtered lord, had collected the thoughts, lusts, terrors, and soul-force of all who'd possessed it over the uncounted ages so that it had a kind of pseudoconsciousness. What he didn't know was that his own brain had been burned with its dark tracks and webs of old and unhuman passion. The thing fought to separate itself from the other two stones that still existed, and from the will of the original maker who schemed from his kingdom at the heart of the world to regain them. The last time he'd tried and failed, Flacchus had been the tortured, unwitting beneficiary. . . .

"Enough play," he said in a firm voice that brought Trivian to attention and froze writhing Beto on the cold floor. "Time is short. I shall give you my commands now."

AT THE OASIS

Antony turned around and saw a slim young man with a sword out in front of him and a robed woman at his side. He felt where the blade had dented the back of his neck above the leather and bronze body armor.

"Should I kill him, Mother?" the boy asked.

"If you still have to ask your dam," Antony said, relaxed now because he didn't think there were any more in the underbrush, "you're not ready for the work."

"No," she said.

"The Romans want to kill us."

"Not this one," said Antony. "I've killed my quota of boys and women for the week."

"I know him," she said.

"That's bad," the Roman said. "When I meet women who know me whom I've forgotten, the next thing is a paternity claim."

"Rest easy," she said, "Marc Antony."

He sighed.

"You know me," he said. And then he realized that he'd done what the voice or vision or whatever it was in the pyramid had demanded, because these had to be the ones he had been sent to find. His next jest went dry in his mouth, and he thought of how all his troubles had really begun long ago at a feast in his own house (he was living with an addermouthed woman whose name he'd blocked forever from memory) when a barbarian soothsayer had killed his pleasure by sending him on a mission to buy the slave girl Bita. He had ended in his lifting her lover, Leitus, from the cross on the Appian Way. He didn't have to ask the woman's name. He knew what it was going to be. He sighed again.

I'll take them with me to Alexandria, he thought, *where they can watch Cleo and myself perish.* With the hope of an empire.

"Marc Antony? The great general?" asked the boy.

"The rich man who's out of funds," said Antony, "is no longer wealthy. It is as if he never was. So with the dead who may as well never have existed."

"What is he saying?" the boy wondered.

"That one defeat cancels all victories," said his mother. "But he's wrong."

Antony yawned and shook a little. The weariness was rising over him like a numbing tide.

"I need to sleep, Bita," he said.

"You know my mother?"

"He's a friend," Bita said. "Though sometimes an unwilling one."

"Better than an enemy," the Roman said.

"You're no friend of mine," Arturus told him.

"I haven't tried to kiss you, have I?" Antony pointed out.

Bita chuckled softly.

Arturus was serious. He'd been educated by a captive people and a father who'd been wronged unspeakably by Rome.

Antony stressed his sight, trying to see more than a blurred female outline.

"I've heard of your perverse Roman practices," he said. "The Lord God with no name who is great will yet smite you all for your sinful ways."

"Peace, Arturus," Bita said, not without amusement. "I said he was a friend."

"Let him be yours, then, Mother," the boy declared, taking a step or two away and turning his back.

Antony sat down heavily on the sand.

"I've ridden long and hard," he said. "We'll talk tomorrow. My head has nothing but sleep in it now." He stretched out. "Then I'll tell you how a god sent me hither to meet you."

"Ah," Bita said.

"Hah!" said her son, not facing them.

"Yes," said Antony, shutting his eyes and dropping away faster than he expected because he thought he was telling them to close the curtains in the great hall of the palace in Alexandria, because the sunlight hurt his eyes and was disturbing the queen's dreams.

"Why do you say a god sent you?" Cleopatra was asking him. "Caesar said he was a god."

"No . . . not like this one. . . . Close those drapes. . . ."

"You were directed here?" Cleopatra seemed to be asking, though he could see she was asleep, her jet hair spilling over the pale pillow, her perfect, almost translucent skin glowing coolly in the sunless morning light. He tried to touch her. He felt sadness and suffering. He felt sorry, so, so sorry. . . .

"Yes," he answered. "I'm sorry. . . ."

He didn't see that Bita (whom he was dreaming was the queen) had knelt beside him, with a small dagger in one hand poked at his bared throat.

"Sorry because you were sent to slay us?" she asked. His face was featureless in the subtle illumination. If the dark ones sent him, then she'd have to kill him at once. She was straining at him with her will, trying to squeeze the truth from his half-dreaming.

"My queen," he said. "Ah, poor Caesar. I loved the man. . . ."

"Were you sent to slay us?"

"Slay? Ah, goddess, I will do as you say and help them escape their enemies. . . ."

And then he opened his eyes as if he felt the pressure of her. He could see both of them where they leaned up and blotted out stars. The boy was holding his sword over him.

"Help who?" he asked.

Antony yawned.

"The unworthy," he said. Yawned again. "Good night. Kill me in the morning." Shut his eyes and let himself go, this time without a single dream between himself and tender oblivion. He didn't hear them still talking.

"Mother?" Arturus asked, the blade still poised. Her dagger had gone back under her robes.

"No," she said. "He's not an enemy."

"He looks like an enemy."

"Don't be prejudiced, Arturus. That's the worst thing to be because all you'll see is what you expect."

He sighed. Let the point drop.

Antony, in the soothing darkness of himself, was alone with an image from the past: in the grape arbor shot with threads of sunlight, about to mount slim, sweet, helpless Bita, and then, at the moment he tried to turn the key in her lock, her voice stunned him, froze his blood and limbs, knocked him back from her . . . just her voice. . . . And then another memory: Leitus staring wildly from inside the cart the gladiator had loaded him into, the bloody, broken hands gripping the sides, straining to say, through parched, swollen lips, through agony and need, that he had to find her, find Bita. . . . And a lost little thought in the dreamless darkness: *It seems he did.*

"I'm afraid for Father," the boy was saying.

"I'm afraid for everyone," she answered. She looked up at the startlingly clear masses of stars and wished they would speak to her, the glowing, lovely ones, the Avalonians.

"This is the hour of war," she told her son. "The gods—the *Elohim,* as the Jews call them—battle with heaven and earth as the stake." To build nothing, to destroy nothing, but just to lift the shadows to let the light in again. And she stared into the sky and saw nothing but the stars that the dark ones hated. Saw nothing to prove anyone was left to fight.

"Heaven is far away, Mother."

"Heaven is at the heart of all things." She hoped, she

hoped. And yet knew. "Only men and gods twist their heart's purpose and dim its glory until they see no light at all . . . and then curse night."

"So the prophets say."

Antony almost surfaced at this point. Had an idea the stars were talking to him, and he liked that. He smiled faintly, like a tender child. He liked the stars talking. . . .

"So we must fight," said Arturus. Somehow he didn't mind that. For all his bent-back studies in dim rooms, his nerves and muscles craved action, longed to ride and strike and battle breast to breast.

Antony sank again, and this time no images streaked his perfect sleep.

ALEXANDRIA

Subius pulled at a flask of wine, sucking the sweetness deep into himself, waiting for soft hands to grip his consciousness. He was pacing along the quay where they were still unloading his ship. Tackle creaked, boxes scraped, men grunted and sweated, cursed and sang.

The day was still hot, hazy, but bright. He felt the difference in the city before actually realizing what was strange.

"Quiet," he said to a seaman dragging a basket of linen across the cracked, yellowish stones, raising a fine dust that hung in the windless afternoon. "Too damned quiet."

The big, long-armed, swarthy man grimaced at him. Grunted. A small, quick, soft-stepping Egyptian in a bright yellow tunic, the harbormaster, looked up from a scroll of numbers and weights.

"Have you not heard?" he called over. The city loomed over them like a white wall.

"Heard what?"

The swarthy sailor stacked the baskets and cocked an ear. His hoop earring glittered.

"The Roman army is coming," the harbormaster said, poring over his scroll. "Many have fled."

Subius wiped his mouth with the back of his hand. He didn't know if the news was good or bad. He kept looking around as if expecting to see Sira with his child.

He thought about getting back on board and staying in his cabin until tomorrow—which would be the soonest he could push the captain into setting sail again. His emotions pulled him back and forth.

He was sure she wouldn't leave the city. She was not one to run. He paced and tried to make up his mind; he wanted to hurry to find her one moment and the next he wanted to run.

About the time he made up his mind to seclude himself on board, he found himself walking up the white stone steps into the city proper.

"It's dangerous," the harbormaster called after him, "for a Roman."

He didn't look back.

"Everything's dangerous," he muttered. He sucked down more wine against the danger. "I have to look at least once upon the face of my child."

He passed a few armed men as he looked for streets he knew. The men watched him but made no moves. He felt but ignored the tension. He had a short sword under his tunic and light cloak.

The city was white, sepulchral. The haze gathered low and close around the buildings, blending them into a series of almost featureless walls.

Like a city of the plague, he thought.

He followed a winding street that gradually slanted down. Most doors and shops were shut tight. Here and there someone flitted past a window.

He paused at the head of an alleyway. Squinted against the haze. He thought something or someone quite large had ducked out of sight down there. Couldn't be sure.

He went around the next bend and finally made out the tower he was looking for. The haze was nearly as dense as fog. By sighting along the position of the tower, all he had to do was count side alleys until he came to the street called Dog.

Almost thirteen years had passed since they'd sat together by lamplight in a public garden overlooking the harbor, sharing a flask of wine. "I'd like you to stay," she'd said, her angular, handsome face leaning into flamelight that softened its edges.

"Ah," he'd responded. "And so would I. . . ." Which wasn't quite true, because he wanted to see a woman who owned two useable ships he coveted. He had additional and obvious reasons for wanting to go to her, except he was one of many, and that was how it would remain. In those days he had ideas about becoming a merchant prince and founding a dynasty with some rich matron. He'd had some luck and luck had made him greedy.

"Then you will stay?" she'd pressed the point.

He'd winced at the night, the sea, and swished some wine around in his mouth as if it had suddenly lost all savor.

"Well," he'd replied, "I have to go back to Italy, but I'll return in a month or so."

Her dark eyes had showed nothing suddenly.

"Yes," she'd said. "Whatever you say."

"It's a matter of business. I'll be back in no time."

He had sensed it had been very important for her, but he'd had no idea why and hadn't wanted to find out. So he'd nodded and felt awkward and let it slip past that first time.

"Whatever you say."

"I'll be back with, I hope, two new ships."

"How nice for you."

"And you too. I mean to have a fleet one of these days."

"May you prosper."

He winced again. He wouldn't ask her what it really was, and she wasn't going to tell him now, and he knew that too. So he went on feeling awkward and foolish until he saw her home, back to the inn of the "Dark Angel"; and when she simply stood in the doorway and said nothing, he moved his hands vaguely. He decided to be outraged and anxious to be away from her company, although the night before he'd basked in the delight of her.

"Your silence proves nothing," he told her, drunken and belligerent.

"Good night, then, Subius."

"Good night, hah. What do you take me for?"

"A Roman."

"I was born in—"

"I know. But I take you for what you've become."

"You weary me, woman," he'd said. "Talk, talk, talk." He already regretted what he was doing. "I'll see you when I return, and then . . ." But he'd lost the thread, and in any case she wasn't paying attention. They weren't looking at each other. She wasn't looking at anything.

How could she not have told me—What did she think I was?

He counted seven streets and then made the left turn. He passed a stall where a few small, bruised, yellowish fruits lay pitiful and isolated on the weathered wood. A fat, barefoot fruit seller with an oiled black beard in tight, Babylonian ringlets glared at him with dark, hard eyes. Two dusky women stood there holding big oil jugs. A soldier tapped his spear on the broken stone paving.

The fruit seller said something biting in Egyptian. Subius understood a certain amount of biting Egyptian. The soldier laughed unpleasantly and stopped tapping his spear haft.

"Peace," said Subius, heading for the corner.

One woman sneered a curse. Subius sighed within himself because the spearman was already moving, saying:

"Wait, Roman pig piss."

I should have changed clothes.

"I am not Roman," Subius said in broken Egyptian. He'd almost reached the corner. He didn't look back as the sandals slip-slapped faster behind him. The women were yelling. He heard the fruit seller's bare feet coming, too, and his grunts. He spun around when something soft thumped off the side of his hairless skull and spattered juice on the dusty white building wall.

"Damn you!" he yelled in Latin.

Someone's always trying to kill me. . . .

He turned at bay because the spearman would have had a free toss at his back in a moment. He didn't think he'd have to draw his blade on this crew. So he waited, crouched in furious suspense and ease despite his mass, which should have been warning enough for anyone with battle sense. In the arena he'd been called "the Great" by the Roman mob. He'd survived wars and revolutions and hated to think of how many men he'd left laced in the blood of their deaths.

But the Egyptian didn't register subtleties, or else was secure in his own skill. He ducked low and thrust up for the center of the big, round target.

He yelled something that Subius assumed was: "Die Roman dog" or the equivalent.

Subius spun like a gravid top. One big hand slapped and stuck to the spear shaft. His speed and strength were a shock. He plucked the spear from the man's hands like a straw from a child's. Then whacked him between the legs with the butt end. The result was satisfying.

Another hurled spear missed him. The women gestured, furious and impotent. The seller backed up, gawking at the fallen fighter, who seemed to be trying to mime the movements of a beached eel.

The gladiator continued on, faster than before. He knew the twists and turns now that led to the inn. It backed on a street behind the palace grounds, which was why he'd had to circle so far around. There was little choice. A stray Roman could not have cut across the gardens and pleasure ponds and walks even if he could have scaled the high white wall.

He sensed he was being followed. Was the soldier contemplating revenge? The wine blurred the edges of his natural caution.

He paused at the door of the small, two-floor, claybrick building that was the inn, the "Dark Angel." He was still sure she hadn't run away. He couldn't imagine her running from anything.

He was suddenly nervous again.

Or should I just turn away and go back? he asked himself.

The inn was silent and seemed closed. The door was shut from inside and the old sign was faded. He hadn't considered that she might have moved away. He sighed, then hit the door with his big fist. It boomed softly. The sound seemed unduly loud in the quiet neighborhood.

He turned around, waiting, thinking maybe no one was there. Half hoping. Reached out the wine and sucked the flask neck. A few drops were left. Disappointing. He sighed and grimaced.

What am I doing here? he asked himself.

And then it was too late, because he heard the door open behind him, stick, bump, and creak. Before he finished turning around, he saw an angular, expressionless face and lean body that seemed to have floated up from the inner dimness, except the work-smooth hand gripping the warped door frame seemed solid as something carved from rock. Even in the shapeless gray garment he noticed her breasts and hips were fuller than he remembered. Soft and full.

"No," she said.

"Wait," he said.

"No," she repeated, but didn't shut the door.

"Let's forget the past." He took a breath. "Let me have a chance to—"

"Why?"

It was suddenly clear to him. His heart had driven him here against his paltry and confused wits. He'd missed her more than any woman in his life and simply hadn't faced it. All the blood and death in his past had taught him to override his heart. His harsh habits had brought him to this, and now his heart was opened and he didn't want to go away. Didn't consider that there might be another man or that she might have lost all interest in him. Didn't bother because that would have taken reason and he was done with reason. He wanted to see his child and embrace this woman.

Why did I wait so long? he thought.

"Please," he said quietly, "let me in, Sira." He hadn't moved, as if she had the strength to keep him from pushing past her. "Where is your uncle?"

"No," she said. "He is dead."

"I want to see my daughter," he said.

"Who told you that?"

"Is it false?" She said nothing. "Please, Sira." He stood immobile as rock. "I offer you all I have."

She didn't exactly snort.

"No doubt you have much. But you are a little late."

He sighed.

"Life is life, woman," he said. "Let the past die."

"Are you so desperate for a child? It's not even a male." She didn't quite sneer.

"I want you."

"I . . ."

"Yes?" He watched her face, her eyes. They were like cool flint in color, yet gentle. She was carefully not looking at him.

"Are you such a prize now?" she asked.

"No. I want you."

"I am married."

He sucked his delicate lips. Let that go past. It seemed to carry no real weight.

"Let the husband come forth, then," he suggested. "Or is he fled?"

He didn't like the idea of the missing years she'd spent with another man and his child. He let it go past him without touching him. He kept his heart open.

"He is fled," she said. "Past all reach."

He understood. That was all right, then. A dead husband.

"Where is my daughter?"

"I have things to do now," she said. She levered herself back into the dark and shut the door without even slamming it.

He sighed and smiled and rubbed his forehead. The sweat was slick.

"Sira," he whispered, facing the door. He was sure

she hadn't locked it. Didn't have to because he was bound to just wait or give up. "What a fool I was."

He sat down on the single cracked-stone step, his back resting on the door.

He stared back the way he'd come. There were a few people standing at the fringe where the haze thickened. He might have thought them phantoms blown from Hades' shores to haunt these doomed streets.

He plucked a thin, dry spear of weed from a clump between his feet and poked it into his mouth. Sucked meditatively. He wondered if he was going to have to sit there overnight. Wished he'd brought a fresh wineskin.

He was sweating a little. The sun was hot, unspecific brightness burning in the blurry sky.

A woman with an empty basket came out of a house across the way, followed by a big black in a loincloth. They stood and pointed at something down the opposite street that he couldn't have seen without getting up and walking halfway to them. After a minute they went back inside.

He puffed out his cheeks and drummed his blunt-tipped fingers on his knees. Shifted around and tried not to think about time passing. A dove with frayed wings landed and fluttered in the dusty street close to him. A grayed, pale dove that flew with a kind of limp. He watched it tip its wings and tilt and wobble around in senseless half-circles, pecking, as best he could tell, at nothing.

He sweated and sat stolid and almost motionless. The bird finally staggered back into the air in a dry gust of dust that hung in a soft churn that gradually sifted down. He sighed. He wasn't sure why.

Somebody was doing something on the opposite roof. He couldn't tell what. He leaned back into the shadow of the lintel. The yard was like a furnace now.

He squinted across the roofline to the south. Noted a dark stain of distant clouds piling up. Must be a huge dust storm out in the desert country, he reasoned idly. Was getting hungry now. Sighed again.

"Sira," he called, facing straight ahead, as if she were across the street. "At least bring me something to drink."

He didn't turn because the blurred figures were coming closer down the street. There were over ten now, he estimated. He was fairly sure the one in front was the soldier.

He cocked an ear. Nothing stirring inside. The line of darkness was coming closer; it couldn't be a sandstorm. The man on the roof opposite was staring at the southern sky now, at dark clouds mounting immensely high. A few gulls wheeled overhead, cutting easy arcs.

Subius pursed his lips and sighed again.

AT THE OASIS

Bita was awake before dawn. She sat cross-legged, her back against one of the palm-tree trunks at the edge of the oasis, facing where the sun would break suddenly above the wide, flat horizon.

The grayish first light was subtle and virtually sourceless. Antony and her son were sleeping. She could hear the man's snores down by the water where he'd dropped off the night before while they were talking to him.

She was breathing slow and deep, concentrating intently. A long, controlled breath . . . she held it, pressing her mind to reach out of her skull, eyes shut tight and focused on her forehead. She tried to force a window to form there (as Abram had called it), a breach in the wall. She tried to reach out without touching the earth with her consciousness. She feared to alert the black watchers below, the unsleeping minions of Aataatana.

She strained as she had in the narrowing ravine when she'd sensed the creatures following them. Reached into immensity until time and space would shimmer and part. Heard nothing now. Felt nothing now. She was desperate and felt so alone. She wanted to save her family. The beautiful, golden people, each one made of gathered dreamstuff pinned and lit by a single jot of sunfire—how could they all have been destroyed? She could not accept that.

So she cried out to them again, called and tried to rip through the dull bone of her head that seemed to wall her within. She tried to touch the fabric of their glory and call them to her.

Her body relaxed until she was totally focused. Time was lost somewhere beyond seas of color and flickering wonder. She relaxed and pressed and called across the gulfs that no human sense explored except in sleep.

Then something gave way, like a crack in a stone, and her forehead ripped as if on a seam, and heaven and earth ripped, too, and she saw the world in the shadowless dreamlight.

Images, past, present, and future, swirled together.

There was a young girl wearing a silky, jet-black hooded robe, sitting on a stool; while someone she had seen somewhere, a bearded Jew in black and silver robes, a crown on his head that reminded her of a basket, stood before her. His eyes moved nervously. Just behind him stood a hard-faced woman who seemed to be a prisoner bound in silver and gold chains, alive with jewelry, almost staggering under the weight when she moved. Behind them blazed bowls of oil and armed men, and she understood this was King Herod and his queen. . . . She heard the words they were saying to each other, but without actual sound, in ripples of the vision substance:

"They plot to unseat you," the hooded girl was saying. "These prophets."

"You need not have troubled to journey so far to tell such things, young Priestess," said the queen. "Things we know quite well ourselves."

"Tell the woman to be still," said the girl. Bita felt her personal force; it seemed cold and distant and somehow more terrible than the simply brutal underlay of the king and his consort. The girl was frightening in her quiet, self-contained manner.

"Be still," said Herod. He was clearly afraid of the girl.

"You are so used to crawling before the Romans," said his wife, "you'll crawl for all."

Herod didn't look as he backhanded her. Hard. Yet the lady barely swayed. Her face stayed set with flinty rage. The girl was talking again:

"They will be warned and try to flee the city. The boy called Isaac they mean to make king of the Jews. Him you must take and bring alive to us. We will aid you."

"King of the Jews," said Herod.

"Yes," she said.

The queen sneered but said nothing. The flamelight gleamed on her massed ornaments.

"Thank you, Priestess," said Herod.

"Alive, you understand?" reiterated the girl.

"Of course, Priestess." He leaned closer as if he feared his own next words. "Will you send your"—brief pause—"minions?"

Her voice was smooth and soft and somehow almost disinterested.

"They are already abroad."

The ripples in the scene intensified until the throne room shook like a banner in a gale and all of them bent and twisted into streakings of darkness . . . and then Bita was gasping air as if she'd nearly drowned.

She was weak and tasted bile as her stomach knotted up. She struggled to rise, but it took her again. She tried to push it away, but it was like shoving a gust of wind. The wind sucked her out of herself and she was again looking at the solid world from the insubstantial one.

This time she saw tall, thin figures, wide in the shoulders and humpbacked, coming across the sands with clumsy, almost limping strides as if walking on the earth were painful. Yet they moved very fast. They were wrapped in pale, mummylike bandages. She realized suddenly that they were fleeing—but from what? They were darting almost like frantic insects. And then she understood: it was the sun! The rising sun. They twisted away from the first light in pain and panic. They hopped over the limp, ripped bodies of the Roman soldiers who had tried to kill her and her son last night.

Why had they lingered so long? She had an impression that they'd paused to eat. But eat what? And then she felt she knew that too. She shuddered. Now they were coming for her and him again—except the sun was searing their strange substance—and then they won their race, reaching the soft dunes just as the golden disc blazed its rim over the horizon and the two of them, with terrific, awkward lunges, dove, clawed, and burrowed under the sand. As the vision shook and fluttered again, there was a flash, an outline limned by the last dreamlight of the shapes under the wrappings, an impression of something hard, shiny, and jet black.

Burning, blinding pain beat at Bita's consciousness as she struggled to draw back from the awful scenes . . . and she lay there, weak, spent in force, with the risen sun blinding her.

"We have to—" she gasped in a whisper—"have to get away."

FLACCHUS

The slave boy lay on the alabaster table, naked. The pale stone was lit by dim lamplight from a hanging ring. The red-edged shadows stirred changing shapes on the bare floor and walls.

Flacchus stood, big, soft, nude, at one head of the table. One incongruously thin, dry-fingered hand rested idly on the boy's bare foot. His thick lips were pursed. His eyes were small and hard like dark pebbles.

Rills of blood had run over the white table and puddled on the marble floor. The boy had been slit from the top of the breastbone to the groin. His arms were stretched out over the table edge like a baby's or a man crucified.

He frowned. Shook his head. A slave boy stood behind him holding a brass bowl, trembling.

"It still sleeps," Flacchus said.

He leaned over and reached into the opened abdomen. The bowl shook in the slender slave's hands so that water slopped over the sides. The fat man groped in the elastic gore and shiny spill of guts. Gripped something. The servant shut his eyes.

It slipped his grip, blood-slick, and he had to grope again. This time he turned his palm and lifted the jet-black sphere to eye level.

"It failed again," he muttered. "There's something I don't know; there's a secret it won't reveal. . . ." He frowned. The part of his mind that was really his own suspected a trap. He knew the master, lord Aataatana, sought this stone and the other two. But he'd assumed he simply wanted them all so that no one else could use them. He wasn't convinced of that now. The surviving Flacchus part of his mind was afraid of being used while the rest, the wild turmoil of ancient lusts and furies and disasters alive in the sphere, had written itself in the rills and channels and dark pools of his brain and was too fragmented to do more than drive him like a ship before an evershifting wind as one collection of desires dominated for a time until another overwhelmed it. The Flacchus part reasoned, but the rest wanted and hated with unimaginable, contorted power. At times it took him over completely, and Flacchus vanished under a feverish nightmare of inexpressible and terrible needs.

Sometimes he thought with distant longing about his past life, his wife and estate, the fine meals they'd had and rides in the country and getting new furniture together for the country villa and evenings caring for his grapes with the old gardener whose name was lost to him. . . . The memories were faded like scrawls of ink on ancient linen.

He sighed and felt the dark desires push his mind as he stared into the stone and saw nothing but the dim flame reflections on the surface. The agonized death was supposed to have shocked the great shadow to stir from the heart of the stone and manifest before him, subject to his will. The ancient memories had taught him each step of ritual. It had failed twice now.

The Flacchus part of him had been driven to take control of the Senate and the armies of Italy. It had been almost a reflex, and he was taught now that it didn't matter. Didn't count. A stir of icy, hard, raging awareness suddenly gripped his mind.

Fool, it seemed to say, *you must possess all the stones; only then can they be opened and the greatness come forth!*

He staggered at the impact. The icy, alien clearness kept focused against the swirling, plural fog of his possessed brain, where shapes rose and dissolved, blown into and out of melting form by the warring minds within him. . . .

He shuddered whenever he recalled the process: lying for unmeasured time beside the black river, locked to the sphere while the composite intelligence it contained soaked into him, floated his feeble, devious personality over its dark depths like oil on water until his self became a mix of all past possessors of the stone. Many of them had not been human. Some had existed and perished before the first human walked the surface of the still partly molten earth, seething in volcanic mists that shrouded vast, amphibious lizards and part-formed primal creatures and a winged, intelligent race with bright, cold eyes like polished onyx. A race that had descended to the slowly cooling world from another far away (so it was said in secret doctrine) and discovered the power sphere on the single solid island in a world of shifting substance. Eventually the sphere came to be cut into three perfect stones.

So the voices and unvoices swirled in his brain, the lost dreams and dreads and furious lusts, babbling, choked, and stunted desires, yanking what was left of Flacchus here and there in fitful starts and stops. But there was a single focus and overriding purpose: to bend all others under him (or them), to press down all things, to squeeze pleasure from all that lived and squeeze the life from life. . . .

His loose lips shook. He brought the stone closer to his face. Felt the cold power seething from it, then pressed it to his opened mouth. It nearly fit as he sucked the blood and tried to suck the coldness, unaware that he was imitating the ritual feeding of a being from a race that had not existed for millions of years but whose essence still lived in the stone.

Memories and pseudo-memories churned: rivers of fire glowing in somber landscapes; jagged mountains where creatures like flattened stones slid and skidded down fiery falls . . . vast open spaces, stars all around, floating over a dark, barren cinder of a world where no flame flickered, sailing through airless void feeling strange fury and measureless grief, dropping down toward a golden-green, misty world bathed in sunlight; then the misty surface, seas without land, fogs that were virtually as thick as the water itself.

He was one and many minds at once: a wizard dancing on a huge black block of broken stone, howling power words into lurid air dense with smoke and fire, raising the sphere in both hands above a multitude packed in among black cube buildings without windows, the people crying out in terror and ecstasy as the rising smoke billowed into a gigantic, winged, and terrible form towering miles high over their ancient, lost city. Another scene: a paffy, soft-limbed aristocrat, ages ago, lying in a shallow silver basin with perfumed, flower-strewn water laving his nude, oiled body while a slim young boy knelt and dipped his face to the lord's sleek groin and prepubescent girls offered various parts of their exquisite bodies to his lips and tongue. Standing over him, straddling his chest, one hand on one hip, was a tanned, slender, perfect-featured boy-girl with tender, firm breasts, torso and limbs curved like a song, and a large, hard glistening penis. The soft lord writhed with delight in the warm bath, the black marble floor awash around him, seeming to suck away the muted light that filtered through hangings and colored glass windows of that pleasure chamber. Another scene: a black armored commander, a king, riding a massive charger up a heap of broken, twisted dead, the setting sun just breaking under a vast, lightning-riddled storm mass that bathed the battlefield in greenish, sickly glare shot with the red sun's bleeding. Around the king, armies were locked in a grinding clash, crunching together as he raised an iron fist to the sky in joyous rage, shouting sweet hate as metal and men screamed and the jet sphere set atop his massive helmet, like an egg in a cup, flashed out dark, deadly beams that tore into the fighters and seemed to force them, like spring-wound toys, to flail insanely together, trampling over pools of blood until they were all smeared with dark red mud. . . .

All these fragments and countless more warred, whirled, contended, in Flacchus' brain and soul like dried leaves in a whirlwind, and he stood there, chewing, licking, foaming, over the sphere, shaking as if electric currents spasmed through his flabby body.

He wanted it. Wanted it all, wanted to suck and devour all the voracious pain and pomp, lust and power. Then, as the images tore through him and he tried to press the too-large stone into his mouth, he screamed, reeled, and fell over the table, the ruined corpse falling with him, the table tipping over under his considerable bulk, the two bodies tangled together as the alabaster shattered on the tile floor.

As the world opened and swallowed him into unconsciousness he reached out with a sense that had never been his own and perceived the present world as if from high above, a sphere of shadow where darknesses gathered in incomprehensible shapes and purposes. He saw where he had to go. There was a point on the shadowy earth, as it might have been viewed by a being of tremendous physical denseness, that seemed more substantial than anyplace else. Power was whirling up there from the solid heart of the world. That was the place to dip the black gem; then the throne, the might, the joy he craved would be his forever. As he lay there in a bloody welter of limbs, entrails, and shattered stone, he screeched and flopped, beating his stubby arms as if they were great wings, arching his back and flapping in the blood.

The young slave's nerve broke. He dropped the rinse bowl and bolted for the door.

AT THE OASIS

Bita was on her feet now as the sun angled through the palm trees. Marc Antony was up, washing his face at the pool.

She went to where her son still lay sleeping. He tossed and struggled and reminded her of when he was an infant. She remembered a time when the three of them were camped on a green slope in a grove of lime trees overlooking a lush valley in the south of Italy. They were then fleeing the country. She and Leitus were sitting at noonday, the sun filtering through the scented leaves and patterning swaddled Arturus with flecks of gold as if he'd been showered with coins. His face was relaxed, lineless in the purest of sleeps. Leitus had looked at him with amazement and a kind of shy delight. The child had suddenly stirred, frowned, struggled, and it was like a darkening of all human innocence and hope. She remembered how the look had irrationally upset her. She had reached out to soothe him instantly.

In the present, she knelt beside her son. Antony (a troubled, sad man, she thought, who saw and felt more than he could ever hope to say and so said things that often cut but, strangely, didn't wound) waved to her, rubbing his face and neck with water.

"Were I inclined to prayer," he called over, "I'd call for a warm bath with suds and a sweet slave to rub me."

Watching her boy in his uneasy dream, she half smiled.

"Rome," she said, "has been enslaved by her slaves."

Antony vigorously smacked his cheeks with both hands, and the droplets sprayed around him, misting rainbows in the fresh sunlight.

Arturus twisted and wrung his hands, trying to get out of his dream. He was sweaty. He was trapped in a dark, stone place, a long, lightless hall. Yet he could see. Someone, *something*, was looking for him. He felt it. He fled slowly, heavily, as if he were a carven figure brought to strange and sullen life.

And he saw with dreamsight into another part of the massive structure where a pale, young, beautiful girl was standing in a corridor blocked by a massive granite block. A short, twisted-looking man in a cowled robe was leaning on a long staff. He seemed to be arguing with the girl. Two very tall, very thin, strangely misshapen assistants wrapped in tight cloths like mummies pressed clawlike hands against the stone as if to shove tons of mass up against the tilt of the passageway where it had obviously jammed fast at the intention of the builders.

He could hear the argument: The robed man was saying that to break the plug would defeat their purpose and loose what they hoped to keep contained, saying they had to bring her brother there first, and she was answering that there was no more time. Then she seemed to gather herself and shout a word, a sound that made the great stones tremble, and then the dream shook, ripped, and he was gasping, awake, blinking at the bright morning just as Antony, refreshed, was saying:

"On a morning like this, I wish I could start my whole life over from the gong." He took a deep breath. Looked around at the sun-laced trees, the bright sand, the sparkling water, and felt suspended in time while the air filled his lungs. Remembered his villa in Italy where he used to walk in the gardens and rest in the grape arbor, drink, eat, and make love to various soft and sweet-bodied women. Why not just go on from here and let the past fade like a dream? Forget the ten thousand causes that were grinding him and his ambitions to dust with their irresistible effects . . . forget . . . start life like a child walking out into the rich joy of morning.

"Are you ill, son?" Bita was asking Arturus.

The boy sat up, shaking his head, breathing hard, rubbing his face.

"No," he said. "Dreams again. . . ."

"The risks of sleep," Antony said. "But I prefer them, lately, to the more substantial of life's disasters." Yet he couldn't help it; just then he felt irrationally hopeful. He kept his mind away from anything but the light and smells and the rested sense of his body.

"We cannot linger here," Bita said. She was cool and serious. Antony could see she was controlling her fear. By daylight she still seemed a girl, though she had to be over thirty now, he estimated. No lines, no marks on her face or stains in her eyes but concern and strain. The boy seemed manly enough. Well, his father had survived the cross that his grandfather had died on. Interesting bloodline and fateline, he thought.

All fighters, even the women, I imagine. . . .

The sweet taste was leaving the day. He thought about what he might have done with a better army or better plans.

"Mother, what's the matter?" Arturus said.

She was heading for the camels tethered in the shade.

"Much," she said. "Hurry."

"I see nothing," Antony put in, peering across the desert.

"You won't until it's too late," she called back.

Arturus went to the water and then behind the bushes while his mother saddled the beasts and the Roman readied his horse.

"What won't I see?" he asked her.

"They'll come as soon as it's dark," she told him. She looked over at her son, who was now squatting behind a tree. "Don't dally."

"I'm hungry," he said.

"Eat as we ride."

"Ride where?" asked Antony.

"To Gizah," she said. "To meet my husband."

"Leitus?"

"Yes."

"I'm going back to Alexandria," he said, sucking his lower lip. "To die."

I followed my madness because I wanted to believe in it, he said to himself, *but sanity strikes at me again, blunt as the sunlight.*

"We can ride together," she suggested, "as far as the Nile."

"Yes," he agreed. "Now tell what you're running from."

She was slightly dizzy. Not faint but vague. The scene floated, drifted, as its substance was thinned and sudden spots and specks of blackness tore at its fabric.

It is back, she told herself. Except she meant she was back in the twilight world herself. She was open again. Now she'd have to face the twilight things again, and worse. The things that lunged out of the eternal night, reached for her, the hands and teeth of darkness.

LEITUS AND BEN YMIR

Leitus kept licking his cracked, sunburned lips. He crouched under the hood of his burnoose, loosely holding the thin riding whisk in one hand. The other was locked on the gathered reins.

He squinted and stared without focus just past the animal's neck. The sand blazed white under the unrelenting sun. They rode, barely speaking now. The heat was sickening. If they didn't reach the river by sunset, there was a good chance they'd never reach anywhere.

Arim Ben Ymir had stopped complaining hours ago. He suffered and tried not to think about anything. He'd blundered, he accepted it, and quietly waited for doom or salvation. He was so numbed and miserable, he almost missed it. The subtle pressure that should have set off his inner alarm. So it wasn't until the first wisping sting of blown sand flicked his face that he turned around and saw the sky had become a brownish gray wall, like a breaking wave, seething, shaking, pounding the desert.

"Lord God of Abraham," he said.

"Can we outrun it?" Leitus called over.

The grinding windsound was already audible and increasing.

"This is bad," said the Jew. "Very bad. But what else? Ai, what else?"

Leitus was alongside of him.

"Do we stop or ride?" he demanded.

"We won't get a mile." He worked his teeth and cracked lips together. "Not a mile."

"You're of vast service, man of the desert," commented the Roman. They were riding toward the sunset, the sandstorm chasing. "We must be nearly across Sinai."

"Unless we strayed," Arim Ben Ymir pointed out. His face showed strain, dark eyes wide and glassy.

The first fingers of driven sand slapped at them.

Arim Ben Ymir was quietly desperate because they were in a long, wide, shallow basin where the sand was packed too hard for cover. "We must ride," he said. They fled with the gathering, gritty gusts at their backs. Their robes tugged and fluttered. In less than half a mile, streamers of dust were closing around them. The clear desert ahead was thickening into a semi-solid churning wall.

"It's upon us," Leitus yelled over the shrilling wind.

"Ride!" responded the Jew. "We must find a lee place or perish!"

The camels were tense, panicked. The men kicked and lashed them. The wind almost lifted them at times. The beasts half spun, staggered sidewise, fled on. The dun-colored fury closed around them.

"Ai! Ai!"

The wind slammed Leitus' mount to its knees. It barely rose again. A few steps more and Ben Ymir vanished into the blasting fury. A swirl hit Leitus and suddenly the camel was gone and he sat on seething air. Rolled over the hard-packed ground, half blinded, choking, thinking in a stunned way that this was like drowning. Felt the same helpless terror as he struggled to surface and draw free breath.

He crawled, gathered his feet under himself, stumbled, spun, lurched like a cripple, ripped clothes snapping as the cyclonic gale booted him down, then up, scraping, bruising, eyes tearing, tight shut.

He skidded, dug in his feet, ran wildly with the gale, nose plugged with sand, spitting in order to breathe. Time was a solid, whirling fury eating him away. He blinked to partly see. And saw a humped shape leap out at him as if taking form from the elemental fury. It slammed into him, and he clutched flesh and hair and held desperately for long seconds before realizing it was one of the camels. Then he discovered Ben Ymir huddled on the lee side of the fallen beast.

The sand was piling up. The Jew had his face part buried under the beast's belly.

Inches apart, Leitus still had to shout:

"Are you alive?"

"Aiii," reacted his companion.

"What?"

"Hellface!" screamed Ben Ymir. "I see you!" He thrashed and tried to drive himself farther under the massive body, which actually was moving under the wind impacts.

Leitus shielded his sore eyes from the blasting grit and glimpsed things, shapes that seemed to fly past, rising and falling in the billows. It was easy to imagine a terrible world of death and fury and demonic vistas as if an army from hell were passing, covered by this impossible storm. Arim Ben Ymir screamed, audible through the muffling camel flesh and the shrieking wind.

And then one, two, three, four figures broke from the wall of slamming sand. Very tall, thin, ungainly yet terrifyingly quick and vital, they seemed to take form from the elemental fury. They leaped at Leitus and the raving Jew.

Leitus had an impression of hard, glossy bodies and long, claw-ended arms. Arim Ben Ymir howled:

"Aiii . . . all the wickedness . . . ai . . . it lives, it takes form . . . aiiiii . . . all hate and dread and nightmare and ill wishes . . . all . . . all gather and sweep over the earth . . . woe unto you all . . . woe . . . for it has taken form and dwells in your abodes! . . . aiiii . . ."

With a thin cry that rasped Leitus' nerves, the tall things leaped for them. Through blurred sight he glimpsed humps like huge folded wings and eyes blazing like molten iron. Ben Ymir went on foaming out his incoherent prophecy.

". . . They come to madden you, O Israel, because they are your children. . . ."

Leitus, crouching against the fearful wind, in reflex drew the long-sword still strapped to his back. The blade flashed in that sickly dimness. In reflex again, he whirled with the ripping wind that had shredded his garments and bloodied his skin. His slashes were like lightning strokes as the heavy sword seemed to swing itself.

Images from fifteen years ago came back to him: the underworld of darkness, vast, basaltic, razor-edged rocks, the black fortress brooding over all, carved from two gigantic mountains, the fitful red glow in the swirling sky of thick, slow night . . . vast stairs . . . winged, stone-hard, glossy demons striking at him as he cut and battered his way to the top of the stairs to reach the pale girl chained to the cracked altar, her pregnant belly bulging, her legs wrenched apart by chains (Bita, it had been Bita) while the vast lord of that vast place swirled down on mile wide wings to claim her fruit and smash him to pieces. . . .

He struck now, sand-slashed eyes useless, seeing only red agony. Struck and scored and twisted with the wind. Felt them scream and fall back, soundless in the contorted fury that dragged him and the Jew along helplessly . . . spun them both faster and faster until there was no time or place and they fell out of the plowing violence into a shock of stillness and silence.

IN THE DESERT

The sun was hot and high over the brilliant, nearly white glare. They'd just crossed the river where it ran wide, flat, and shallow that time of the year.

Arturus turned in the saddle, staring at the gigantic sandstorm that cut the horizon in half to the north, churning over the Nile and heading west, parallel to their direction.

Bita rode calmly, sensing things that weren't exactly visible. It was as if she looked through a lens of smoky crystal. Other, subtler worlds were starting to come between her and the solid landscape again. As it had been fifteen years ago. There was, she knew, a price to pay for the altered vision. She would have liked to escape somewhere and live what she called "a little life." Live in peace and enjoy her family. Perhaps have a second child. Forget all mystery and prophecy. All strange powers and wars.

Through the lens the blunt facts shimmered in the way heat waves shook and blurred the desert surface and bent and melted the trees along the blue-bright sheen of the river.

I have chosen it this time, she told herself, *and I think I'm alone in it this time.* She didn't look at the storm mass that was like a miles-high wall between them and Alexandria, by Antony's best reckoning. He'd decided to stay with them a little longer. The end could still wait.

Maybe, he thought, amused, *my men are still looking for me at the pyramid.* He was putting off the end, he decided, like a boy in trouble taking the long way home.

Bita didn't watch the storm because she was gathering her quiet. She rode with folded hands, gathering herself to listen. She felt shadowy things stirring in that storm, questing, fitful, hungry beings, hunters. She suspected that if she prayed there, they'd feel her and come for her. So she listened and tried to radiate nothing.

With her eyes nearly shut, the shadowy things thickened and she had glimpses of shafts of darkness spilling from the storm center and reaching across the desert, dimming the pure sunlight. These shafts flicked over them and she registered a chill and felt a consciousness in the cloud. She recognized it: that keen, cold, immeasurably old intelligence with a pride and power incomprehensible to mortals, and she understood that it was sustained on the surface world by the forces in the heart of that unnatural fury of wind-knotted sand. When the storm died, that questing, coldly furious mind would simply regather itself in the dense depths where it lived and ruled.

"There," said Antony, pointing ahead where the pyramid tops just showed, cutting neat chips from the shimmering western horizon.

"Let's make all haste," Bita said. She was suddenly exhausted, and it showed in her voice. Antony was concerned. She was pale and slumped in her seat between the dromedary's hump.

"Are you ill?" he wondered. "Perhaps the sun . . . ?"

"No," she said, holding on while the desert reeled and black flashes opened the sand like pits. She was afraid that the animal was going to stumble in and they'd be lost and drop down to the nameless world, where she'd exist as a fragile ghost blown through the thick darkness by the dense desires of the hard, harsh masters.

"Haste," she repeated. Because the beams were flicking past them now, rapidly gaining, and she perceived, in a nauseous vision, the swirling forces and spinning pools of energy that actually opened the pits like lacunae in a heat mirage.

No, she thought, very dizzy now, afraid she wouldn't be able to hold on until they reached the pyramids. Not that she believed they'd be safe there, but she simply wouldn't try to think past that.

"The storm," she said. "The storm is turning this way." The dark rays reached out like stylized carvings on a tomb wall.

"Jupiter's dick," said Antony, "she's right."

He watched the vast, towering, fuming mass ponderously swinging around and billowing in their direction. He had what he took for an irrational moment, imagining the storm was actually seeking them like a hunting creature.

They lashed their mounts along. Bita wobbled and clutched the long, bobbing neck.

I have to resist, she told herself. *I cannot let it sense me . . . cannot . . .*

Arturus exulted in the awesome power of the storm with only a vague notion of the danger. He was riding out in front and was unaware of his mother's distress.

I think, Antony said to himself, *if I'm going to have to go inside that damned tomb again, I'd do better to perish in the sand because I'm going to have to end it soon, in any case, and it's just a Roman's choice of where.* He realized that meant something to him. He was still a Roman. He liked many of his people's ways. He took them for truths. Far, far less than when he was a youth, but being a Roman now was going to make the last act easier. *But I still must see her first. I refuse to leave that undone. May the gods help her, may they please help her because I love her and it's hopeless. Hopeless and damned. But I love her.* Even the Roman part of him admitted it. *It's always too late; everything was always too late. . . .*

Bita, eyes shut now, brought the dark forces into sharper focus. Each jet-dark beam had a clawed hand at the end with talonlike, red-gleaming nails. She remembered these things and shuddered. It was the same nightmare again. Nothing had improved; in fact, without the golden people, it was infinitely worse, and there was despair in her fear this time. One of those hands had held her in the stifling underlands, had struck at her while she was sweeping the hut in Lirium when she and Leitus and the big gladiator Subius Magnus had been hiding from the power of Rome, when she had been Leitus' slave, given to him by his treacherous uncle, Flacchus. Then a golden brilliance had blocked the deadly blow and she'd heard the golden voices of the now (she feared) forever lost beings of glorious Avalon.

As she wobbled in a partial faint, her coppery hair fallen loose from her hood, her lovely oval face pale as polished alabaster, she saw into the storm, even as she strained not to look, and glimpsed the shifting outlines of a winged, vaguely human shape. A shape she recognized. A form that any mortal would know had he never seen even a crude picture of anything like it: thin, with a long face, long, slender limbs, gleaming, lipless, with slit eyes like fanned coals, eyes that hurt and burned what they looked at. A shape from the lightless heart of universal nightmare. It had gloated over her when she lay in its power.

She realized that it was more than solid, that at the center of that ferocious, magical storm was a core of denseness, the very semi-solid atmosphere of the abyss. Aataatana, she knew the shape was called. Lord Aataatana. His powers were growing. A voice that might have been her own wild and feverish mind was saying as she wobbled in and out of consciousness: *Aataatana has disordered that which seals the worlds. The worlds are all growing heavy and losing their color. If he succeeds in making the three into one again, the three dark stones that were once a single dread shape, then the light will die, too, and the last flame and hope of all creation will be squeezed into dull muck. . . .*

She believed she felt the red stare and the snarl of recognition and delight. It was a wave of nausea. She reeled and nearly fainted in sick disgust.

"Mother," called Arturus. "What's wrong?"

The first curls of wind stung them. The camels rocked and slipped and skidded over the dunes.

She kept pushing against the nauseating black weight. Gasped burning air. Resisted the pressure that was forcing her out of herself into a dimension where she would be more vulnerable to the non-physical forces.

She held on. The pits opened around her. The dark talons clutched and it was as if the whole mass of the storm were leaning down to snuff her out.

The great pyramid loomed over them at last, the ancient, weathered stones and fragments of shattered casing reflecting the terrific sunlight.

She fought and cried out for help as the sand-cyclone closed over them, tearing and blinding, and the darkness leaned down on pinions of power and terror. . . .

LEITUS AND BEN YMIR

They'd half run, half fallen in tandem, spun by the contorted wind, Leitus still slashing at the thin shapes but seeing nothing but pain and redness blurring. He didn't grasp that he'd struck water until they'd both surfaced, sucking air and choking on sand that hissed and beat the river surface to turgid froth.

"Ai," sputtered Arim Ben Ymir. "Lord, save Thy servant."

Leitus was gripping him with desperate strength. Ben Ymir felt it was God's hand upon him. It gave him courage as he struggled to swim, and the current swung them out into the channel. There was no visibility. The sand rained down like the unleashed malice of fate as he thrashed ineptly in no direction.

But the hand gripping his arm comforted him. He knew he could not be truly lost. It was as if the water itself flowed through his body and healed him. The wild storm held no terrors now. He would not die until he had spoken out. The water promised this to him. So that not in fear but in fury he would tell them all their folly and announce the dread they'd brought upon themselves. Upon Israel.

Leitus was a strong swimmer (he used to cross the Tiber in Rome at the great bend), and was actually supporting the flailing Jew, who otherwise would have gone under. Leitus saw only redness, but he managed to sheath the sword on the third try. He assumed that Ben Ymir was leading him. Ben Ymir was certainly speaking, panting, blowing water, but talking incomprehensibly and at a great rate. Praying, it sounded like.

The hand of God guided Ben Ymir effortlessly and upheld him. He was content and kept the praises flowing from his lips and the promises, too, of what he would do, how he would travel about and bring the word of truth to all Israel. Sometimes he spoke under the surface and the words were bubbles. Other times the sand ate them.

"Which side are we near?" Leitus asked. He had to reach the pyramids to find his family. "Which side?" He kept twisting his face in the water, trying to clear his sight. Every blink was a needle-rip, eyes clogged and gritty.

God of the Jews, he thought, *don't let me be blind! Please . . . please.*

The lids were swelling shut.

Ben Ymir kicked and thrashed about aimlessly with utter confidence.

"The Lord has upheld me in the dread hour," he was saying. "The Lord guides my feet on the dark paths."

The air had cleared. The storm had veered away. The sun was dipping down into the west.

Ben Ymir was still talking, Leitus still swimming with one arm and both legs. He was trying not to think about being blind. He'd given up asking Ben Ymir questions.

Ben Ymir was not surprised when they were suddenly walking in sandy mud. A curved bar had plucked them from the current.

"Are we across?" Leitus couldn't help but ask as the Jew pulled free and staggered from the water.

"Praise His name!" he cried. "Praise His name!"

Leitus followed his voice and slosh of garments and the slope of the bank, one hand stretched out before him, now and then touching the other man, who was punctuating his songs of deliverance with sounds of pain.

"Which side are we on?" Leitus asked. His eyes were swollen tight and sealed with burning pain. Panic nosed at him like a killer shark.

"The side of the Lord God of Hosts," replied the Jew.

Leitus lost contact. He waded up and out, high-stepping forward, and then the ground tilted away on the reverse slope and he fell flat in the shallow water again. How could he have turned around? Of course he hadn't; he'd simply stumbled over the other side of the bar.

He splashed out again, feeling disoriented. He pressed his hands to his eyes and didn't quite shout:

"Dung and slime!" Staggered. "Oh, now meaningless!" Pounded his head in a frenzy while his little companion bowed and waved his arms, staring at the wide riverflow, seeing immense things, apocalypses, burning blood and universal night falling like heavy smoke from a ruined sky.

The Jew led him along the soft spine of mud and sand to the actual shore. Leitus tilted his head back in frustration and misery, his swollen, sand-ravaged eyes turned skyward as if in prayer, leaking burning tears.

"I look upon your cities, O Israel," declaimed Arim Ben Ymir, "and I smell the rank dead and hear the lamentations of your children."

"Now I have lost everything," said Leitus. He used the scabbarded sword as a stick now to grope his way behind the Jew. Shadows ran flat and long as the sun set. The light was like golden-tinted blood on the water. "Oh, I wish there were truly gods, that I might meet them after death and wring their necks!"

"There are gods," said the Jew, "yet the Lord scatters them like chaff when the flail beats the wheat." He smiled with pleasure and satisfaction and calm certainty.

Leitus wept and spat. "Idiot," he said. "Superstitious fool. What Lord? What gods? We are ruled by blind fate and happenstance. Our deaths mean nothing —and I have no luck—none."

Lumps of walking meat, he thought, *waiting for the butcher's stroke. . . .*

They followed a faint footpath that wound along the riverbank. Their shadows spilled across the sand, throwing their movements into huge, discoordinated abstractions.

"Pain is my boon companion," said Arim Ben Ymir. "The Lord has marked me out for my sins. I have read no holy books, yet all that is written is known to me now." The little Jew squinted as the sun fell behind the horizon as behind a dark wall, and the blood-colored wash went darker like clotting. He thought he saw the tallest towers of the city in the last glimmer of twilight.

"Take heart, Leitus," the Roman told himself, "the Lord of the Jews will succor you yet." He didn't smile. He clutched his end of the sword and followed where Ben Ymir led.

It was suddenly night. The stars were sharp and hard.

Oh, Bita and my son, he thought, *I will soon be dead and gone. . . . All I have known and done will be lost like water into sand, and you will never know my precious moments—nor will I know yours. The world has closed me in. Ah, I've been walled into myself like a prisoner into the deepest dungeon, and there is nothing now but blankness.*

"Nothing," he said. "Nothing at all."

CLEOPATRA

Sunset. The city seemed joined to the sky by a seam of fire. Naiar was looking for the queen. He crossed the polished deck of the royal barge, which was still moored before the palace. He didn't actually believe that there was enough crew left on board to sail the ship; he simply didn't let the thought arise. There would have to be enough, so there would be enough.

In the torchlight the few slaves he saw looked morose, like animals before a storm broke. The unnatural silence here and in the city oppressed him.

At the cabin hatchway a giant Nubian guard leaned on his spear. He was one of Antony's men.

"Where is your mistress?" Naiar demanded. He could imagine the faintly contemptuous expression on the long black face, almost invisible in the shadows.

"Below," said the guard, after the slightest pause, with nothing one way or another in his tone.

Naiar brushed past the man and went down the steps.

"Don't be surprised," he said over his shoulder, "if we set sail."

Because he'd made up his mind. He was going to tell her and then give the orders himself.

He stepped into her quarters without knocking. Two young girls watched him with big, worried eyes as he entered. She was across the cabin, alone in dim light, sitting at a gilt in-wrought table. The polished surface gleamed like something seen underwater. Her pale hands were resting on the dark wood. She'd just set out a row of jeweled plaques with inlaid designs that seemed like arrows and flowers.

He paused a step from the table but gave the impression he was still racing ahead. She didn't look up. He barely noticed that she'd loaded her body with massive beaten-gold circlets, necklaces, bracelets, rings, a thick tiara, and a magnificent spun gold robe. He might have wondered how she would actually stand up under the weight, because it hadn't hit him that she was dressed for her interment.

"Naiar," she said. "I never believed in the gods until they turned against me."

He blinked, still seeming to rush forward, seeming stunned to a temporary stop.

"You are a priestess," he said, not because it was particularly important, but simply in response, to start talking. "I—"

She cut him short.

"One of my countrymen said no one reaches old age without coming to believe in the gods."

"Queen, I—"

"The gods are real," she said, not looking up.

He was studying the array on the table. The gold leaf had been worked in stars and suns, and in the center was a white-gold crescent moon. He stared at the plaque, which indicated the outcome of events according to the divining system she was using.

"Do you trust these symbols?" he asked her.

She didn't look up. "The gods move the hands that move the images of truth," she said.

"Do you understand the outcome before you?" He meant the last symbol, the shattered chariot.

"Yes," she said. "Why do you come to vex me, Naiar?" She raised one strong-boned hand and let it fall back lightly. "Let me come to the unraveling my own way."

"Dreaming that the Roman will save you?"

"Nothing can save me."

"I want you to give a command. Or I will."

"You had better, because I'm finished with commands. And there are few left to heed them."

He realized she wasn't looking at anything. He stood there, stopped in frozen, pent-up, almost hysterical motion. First he'd given up his vows, then his future, and now there was nothing but shadows, a lost woman, a lost cause, a dying hope. And love. He couldn't forget love.

He wanted to put his hands on her and shake her, pull her violently out of it, her life, her doom, the shadows that had sapped everything.

He rubbed his shaven skull, searching for words and a way. Because he saw it now so clearly: he'd put on the robes of a priest, learned the rituals the way a warrior learned to cut and thrust and a fisherman to tie knots and cast his nets. As a child they were all taught, he realized, what pleased the world and what it hated. Learned to discipline the heart and stifle the child within. She had learned to be queen. They'd chained her to it. But, he saw, the child was still under all the weight of their buildings.

They had to cast off everything and start fresh, and in the pouch at his belt was what he believed to be the means. Desperate means. He'd gone under the main temple the night before. Many of the priests and guardians of the sacred places were away, hiding holy and valuable items from the oncoming army, so it was not hard for him to sneak into the forbidden area, down the circular stairs to the lowest level, where vast and secret statues in the high-roofed cavern, which predated the founding of the city by uncounted ages, brooded over flaming braziers of oil that were never allowed to die out. He felt small as a mouse at their vast feet. The black, shiny stone they were carved from seemed to suck away the uncertain light. The secret gods who would unmake creation.

He'd been taken down there once by the elder priests to be initiated into the knowledge of annihilation, the wisdom that would terrify him into smallness.

Last night he'd crouched in the massive shadows of the caverns that underlay the entire world with hidden exits in every country, and if he'd been caught there, it would have meant death without appeal. But he hadn't been caught, and he had the drug in his pouch stolen from the arsenal of Anubis.

"We must cast off what we have been," he insisted. "We must!"

She pursed her lips, staring across the cabin at the place where the two slave girls crouched, watchful and afraid.

She touched the first plaque in the sequence: flowers, stars, and crowns. Sighed faintly.

"Could I but go back to those days," she murmured.

He was shaking his head.

"No," he said. "That's wrong, don't you understand? We must forget and be born again." He blinked too fast, too hard. "He's not coming back to you. He's dead," he suddenly told her. "I'm giving the order to sail. I'm giving the order."

She poked another richly worked plaque, still not looking at anything.

"Sail where?" she wondered. "Poor Naiar."

He trembled. Chewed his lower lip. He wanted to shout.

"Upriver," he said. "Out of the Roman grasp."

"I never seem to be outside of that." She was relaxed now. He understood that she'd accepted it. "I know he's dead. I've just not been quite ready, you see." Because the years were all there, vivid, whispering through her memory like the falling leaves in the countries of winter. "I didn't think I loved him," she whispered. "I thought it was good policy. I thought . . ." Because she hadn't had to love Caesar. He was her protector and teacher, and it ended with her teaching him some things. "I didn't think I loved him."

"I'm going to order the captain to sail."

She shrugged. "I am already dead. You can take this body where it pleases you."

"You have to forget," he tried again, panic and

despair showing. "You have to."

"There's little doubt I will," she assured him. "Poor, poor Antony."

"Poor!" He sighed and rubbed his face. Thought about how to get the drug into the wine. He could promise her oblivion without pain. Yes. He could. And then take the drug himself once they were safe. Like two newborn babes, they would discover one another and life at once, together. "Poor, indeed. Poor to you and his own Roman wife. Driven to love you by politics alone. Poor in battle. He's destroyed everything."

He clenched his fists. Bit his lips. A dark seam of blood creased his chin.

AT THE PYRAMID

Bita was so sick, she couldn't walk after dismounting at the base of the immense structure. Antony and Arturus half carried her into the temporary lee of the great stones.

The storm stood over them as the light failed, so that when Arturus glanced up, billows and columns of sand were shot with shadows and deep red sunset fire. The feet of the storm were claws of sand-cloud that tore ground and air and lashed against the pyramid as they scrambled to find a way inside.

"Last time," Antony was saying over the mounting howl and rush, "it was easy."

They lifted her up to the third level of masonry.

"There's no doorway," Arturus called to Antony, crouching against the gathering gale, moving along the line of massive granite blocks. Antony followed with Bita slung over one shoulder. His leg muscles burned from the strain.

"Keep going," he told the boy. Cleopatra had told him a way had been opened on the third tier. *If we don't get in, we will die,* he thought. *Except for the fact that I'm a walking corpse as it is, so as soon as the storm lets up I'll leave them and go take the tenth place in line. . . .* Meaning he would stand where the first man to be killed stood when a legion was decimated for some grave offense. In a sense he was almost looking forward to the end now. He kept the blankness in reserve against the agony and despair that lay like a black wall across every road open to him.

A swirl of sand clutched at them like a hollow hand. They swayed. Arturus gripped a crack in the stone. Antony leaned in.

The block the boy held pivoted smoothly, and there was an opening.

In fact, Antony thought, *I've known whorehouses harder to enter than this mighty pile.*

The wind slammed them against the granite, and he almost fell before staggering into the opening. A last slap of sand-wind blinded him for a moment. They stood in a slanted, solid corridor.

The wind blasted and screamed across the opening. The pressure sucked at them. The sand hissed and clattered inside. Outside was just dark fury now.

Arturus heaved the block back into place, but it stuck partly open, grinding on the accumulated sand.

They sat, Bita across Antony's lap, against the wall in lurid semidarkness.

"Well," said Arturus, "we're pretty safe now, I suppose."

And then he saw the error in that notion, because a pair of too-long, shiny black taloned hands reached around the edge of the massive block and began to heave it open. The grit in the crevices that should have jammed it crunched and squealed.

Antony stared, then set Bita aside and drew his sword. Knelt over and chopped at the glossy wrist, which suggested beetle skin, in a reflex of fear and fury.

"Unnatural monster!" he hissed.

It was as if he'd hit just the stone. The impact jarred his arm. The claw held.

Arturus came up, his own blade poised.

"I'll hew it," he said, excited.

"Never mind," said the Roman. "Fall back. It's a thing unnatural. Back!"

The pivot stone stuck, rasped another few inches. Antony was already picking Bita up again. She was partly conscious now and managed to stagger along with him as they half ran down the corridor. Arturus followed, reluctant, thinking about striking at least one blow on his own at the thing.

The slope was sharp. Pitch black. At any moment Antony expected to plunge into some pit or slam into a dead end. He heard the stone above them grind and crash open dully.

And then there was sudden torchlight coming from an upward slant. They skidded to a halt. He stood panting, holding Bita upright like a child. She stirred and murmured.

They faced a giant step where one branch of the corridor sloped up while the first went down through an arch into blackness.

The flameshadows, for an instant, gave Antony an impression of a man formed of soft light with a stern, compassionate expression holding back a flood of darkness. For a fraction of time he stared into the sudden flameglow with wonder and inner calm.

And then everything was moving too fast again: quick footsteps clacking down the corridor behind them; a cry almost too high to hear, a shrilling that hurt his head. Bita opened her eyes, gasping:

"O lady of light, save us!"

Because immensity loomed, squatted on the capstone of the pyramid, wearing the stormfury for a robe, standing at least a mile high, great taloned feet pressing down even the titanic weight of earth's greatest construction. The immensity's eyes were red violence. They probed down into the stone that it could not penetrate in its present form. There was energy in the stones, invisible to ordinary sight, that kept it at bay.

Antony was staring at a pale, lovely girl who must have been fifteen or sixteen at best. She wore a robe that hid her feet. Her hair was lustrous and jet black. One hand was under the folds of her garments.

She somehow reminded him of Bita when he'd met her fifteen years ago. Except he was instantly afraid of her and not of the twisted one-armed old man who'd just limped out beside her, leaning on his long staff, tilting his head like a blind man.

He sensed others around them in the dark passages. Behind her a large granite block seemed to have been shattered. Broken stone was heaped around them. Obviously the upward way had been blocked.

All this in an instant with the footsteps coming behind them, the sudden torch flare, Bita crying out and his own voice shouting to the boy:

"Follow me!"

And running for the downslope archway. Except the girl in black said:

"Stop."

And he and Arturus did, as if they'd hit a wall. For an instant their limbs locked. They staggered and went down. Bita rolled out of Antony's arms. She knew that trick, she was thinking. She could have done the same thing with a little practice.

And then she realized the girl hadn't even aimed it at them. A seven-foot-tall figure wrapped like a mummy, with too-long arms that ended in steely, black claws, long head bound like the victim of some hideous wound, with a big, lumpy back, stood frozen in the entrance they'd just come out of. That was what had been chasing them. The long, thin arms gripped savagely at nothing.

Antony rose to one knee, saw another tall, inhuman figure in the downward passage also. They'd have been in his arms in an instant.

Bita stood up. The weakness had passed. Arturus followed suit, sword ready.

The girl in black was talking to them now, in Hebrew:

"You may as well come peacefully. My servants will detain you in any case."

"Come where?" asked Bita sharply. She gathered herself, collected her inner force. This was the girl she had seen in her vision of King Herod's court. Recognizing the accent, she said in her Briton dialect: "Child of evil."

"You are harsh, Aunt." The girl didn't exactly smile.

Stayed in Hebrew, which left Antony out. Arturus had been taught his mother's original tongue, along with Latin and Greek.

"Aunt?" he echoed.

"Yes, Cousin. Bridegroom." Now she was smiling faintly. Her voice was soft and remote. "Or ought I say Brother?"

"Brother?" wondered Bita, trying to maintain her concentration. Antony was still gaping at the strange clawed creature.

"Who are you, child?" she went on in dialect. "I know only the darkness that shrouds your heart and the black servants who wait on your bidding."

The blind priest Cavul lurched a half-pace nearer the edge of the great step. He gripped his staff fiercely.

Antony was looking for someplace to run.

"A family reunion," said Cavul. "We must lose no time."

The dark girl seemed unhurried.

"Cannot you hear the storm without?" she asked. There was no sound at all in there, of course. "Why hurry me?" She looked at him without expression. Then, to Bita and her son: "Mother and bridegroom, I have decided to go to the end. I was minded to quit and leave them all to rot in their prophecies." She shrugged slightly. The silky robe shimmered in the flameglow. "But where could I go and what would I do there? They've ruined me for ordinary life. I hate them. But I have none to love." She shrugged again. One hand stayed inside the robe as if holding a secret wound. The tall thing stayed frozen in mid-rending. "So I will make them pay the price for the power I will bring them. They will regret it, I think." She almost smiled again. "Yet, this one is not to be trusted. And he is exactly like the rest." She looked down at Arturus. "He wants me to go out into the storm he pretends not to hear. Now, why is that?"

Cavul tilted his head.

"What are you saying, Morga?"

"That you hope to betray me," she said, looking at Arturus. "Come to me, my brother."

Bita controlled her breath carefully. Waiting. Knowing she wasn't strong enough yet, but ready to fight. She felt crisis gathering in there like thunderstorm air before it breaks.

And then the tall, awkward, taloned servant moved again. Hunched into the branched corridor.

"I did not bid you approach me," said Morga.

The creature made a sound that was like steel grating on stone. Then it came forward another long, wiry, hunching step.

Morga shouted in the same language. Bita knew the sounds, though not the meaning. She'd heard it in her mind in visions and in the underworld itself. It was plain the girl in black was shouting *stop*. Equally, that the long, deadly, humpbacked thing wasn't stopping. She was surprised. They were obviously supposed to obey.

Bita perceived a dark swirling in the close, smoky air. Something like a shadowy hand groped, then closed long, blurry fingers around the crippled priest. He thrashed for a moment. The stick flailed, then snapped in his grip.

Another one with falling-sickness, Antony thought.

Morga aimed her right hand (the left still buried under the folds in her shimmery garment) as if it were a weapon at the advancing, birdlike monster. She yelled in the spondaic tongue and the being was checked again. Its wrappings burst and a huge pair of glossy wings like hardened leather crashed and creaked, swirling the close, smoky air and billowing the torches into a roar. It shrilled a sound that hurt nerves and bones. Arturus clapped his hands over his ears, though it did little good.

Morga kept her long middle finger pointed at the thing, and it stayed still as if suspended there by an invisible pin.

Next the one-armed priest shrieked in a voice that seemed far too big for his throat. The sounds seemed to be bursting him asunder as he spoke. Blood ran from his nose and mouth so that the words bled from his lips. Part of the shouting was in Briton speech familiar to Morga and Bita; part in the dread language that, while utterly unfamiliar, seemed perfectly clear.

"I am come for what is mine!" the priest cried out, body thrashing like a fish on an unseen line, chest puffing like a croaking frog. "I am come! Deliver up what is mine!" Blood dribbled and sprayed. Blind eyes stared knowingly.

It's as if his chest is a blacksmith's bellows, Antony thought. *And someone is pumping it to make speaking wind.*

Not releasing her mysterious check on the winged monster, Morga demanded:

"Who speaks to me?"

Bita had just noticed a second creature waiting in the shadows of the downward slope just beyond the archway.

"This rag," said what had been Cavul, the chest and belly squeezing in violently so that the words were a bark and sounded to the amazed and unsure Arturus like: *Naaa'y at' thhh.* "But I am I. You are mine, my daughter. My own." Blood misted from mouth and nose. The sightless sockets leaked crimson. The dead priest seemed to be held upright as if the pinched shoulders were gripped by unseen fingers.

Bita stayed braced inwardly, all her strength gathered to resist when the moment might present itself.

I must save my boy, she thought. She understood he was swept up by sheer wonder. At his age he'd have to be; here were genuine devils and wizards. Not dull Talmudic studies. In fact, Arturus had an idea that the Lord God or one of his holy minions would soon spear any real darkdoer with a shaft of sacred light when and if the situation demanded it. There wasn't time to be afraid yet. For Marc Antony there was just too much to take in. He was trying to convince himself that coming inside here had brought back the strange fever. Because this scene was past assimilating. And since he knew he'd never go mad, he was stuck with it, like an amputee on the battlefield awake under the surgeon's saw.

"You are my father, are you?" Morga asked. Her finger stayed pointed.

"Yes," uttered the bleeding rag. The legs hung twisted and limp, yet it seemed to stand. "Obey me."

"You never taught me that," she said. "But you're not my brother's father, too, are you?" She grinned. "Come inside here to me," she insisted, "yourself." She paused. "Father."

"You know I cannot. Come forth to me!" He boomed this and ruptured the throat of his speaking corpse. The neck puffed out and sagged like a frog's sac.

"No," she murmured.

The words shook blood from the dead one.

"Bring your brother and his mother." The robes had fallen away. Now the thin ribs cracked and rippled.

"No, Father. If that you truly are, I have no cause to love you."

"Who asked you to love?" The thundering voice heaved the ruined bladder. "I command you to obey."

"No," she said again. "Go away, Father. Stay in your hole. I have had no life at all. I ask for none now. But I shall rule nations in this world and plug you up in yours. Father."

Perhaps the percussive sound the dead, flopping thing next made was meant to be laughter.

Antony shuddered as gore exploded everywhere, spattering them all. The girl never broke her concentration on the winged being who seemed to be straining against an invisible wall.

"Ugh," said Arturus, as the empty shell of the priest flopped down and there were no more words.

"I've won," said Morga to Bita and Arturus, in Briton speech. "You'll both come home with me now."

"Home?" wondered the boy.

"Yes. I don't intend to slay you, Brother. You are fair of face, I see. As I am, myself. Not that vanity is a problem with me. No more than feeling." She'd just switched to Hebrew, as if it amused her. She still held her hand up as if casually to hold the creature at bay. She was smiling.

SUBIUS

Subius stood up. The vast storm filled about half the southern sky. Some of the few people still in the city were out in the streets or on rooftops, watching.

He peered along the street at where whoever they were still stood watching at the borders of the haziness as if watching or waiting for him.

"Enough," he muttered, then reached for the doorhandle. And he always was to wonder if she hadn't been standing there all the time, watching him sit through a space in the boards, because she opened it just ahead of his hand.

"Where is your uncle?" he found himself asking, for some reason.

"Dead," she said.

"Are you alone here?"

She shrugged.

"Myself and my daughter."

He nodded.

"I've made up my mind," he said, looking hard at her from under his jutting brows. He stood solidly and seemed as immovable as a granite statue. Emotionally he was stumbling forward, saying: "I want to tell you that I've made up my mind."

"Very well," she said.

"So you had better . . . what?"

"Very well." She wasn't even smiling. Her eyes were careful, amused yet serious.

"Very well what?"

"Come in."

He hesitated. "Yes," he said, to no point.

"Aren't you hungry or thirsty?"

He nodded.

"Come in and meet your daughter."

LEITUS AND BEN YMIR

Leitus felt the coolness and knew they were suddenly under shade. He wondered if it were trees or buildings. It had to be noon, he believed, because the terrific sun-pressure had been slamming straight down on his bare head.

At least I can tell day from night, he said to himself. He was holding a fold of his companion's rent cloak to guide himself. The fine dry dust of the road irritated his nostrils and caked on his lips. He kept wetting them, but the chapping was raw and stung.

They were making sharp turns, and he heard voices now. They had to be in the city. The rosy, misty brightness shut his sight down like a wall across his eyes. Last night he'd been unable to sleep much. He'd been troubled by vivid images from the past. Claudia's body, his lover over fifteen years before who'd been horribly murdered by her brother Iro in Rome . . . Leitus had been obsessed and besotted with her . . . and all night he'd kept trying to understand why all these things had happened to him. Why? It seemed so purposeless and cruel. . . . Kept seeing the blood spatter and stain that had laced the lovely, smooth, nude body. And thought, more wildly as the day wore along, that there might as well have been a message in that crimson scribble saying Leitus, you are lost, you will be an exile in strange lands and lose all you had without reason or meaning, just ill fortune, and there will be no end until you are sucked forever into the final darkness. . . .

Why is the city so quiet? he wondered.

"Where have we come to?" he asked the Jew.

"To the place of the dead" was the useful reply. "Yes, to the whitened tomb itself."

"Alexandria?"

"What matter names to the dead?"

A blind man and a madman, Leitus thought. *A fine pair.*

"Speak plainly," Leitus tried. "Mock not the blind."

"You are all as the blind." They took what had to be a corner, and Leitus heard more voices. Someone, a man, was shouting and seemed to be running as he shouted, his words swallowed by other words, echoing. Then screams back behind them. Horses neighing. Crashes that might have been the clash of arms.

Sounds were like shapes to him now. But apart from that, everything seemed like everywhere else. Except the smells. Yes, he couldn't forget the smells. And the shade and heat. And wetness. Yet it seemed that one place was really like another.

"Where are we now?" Leitus asked. He thought he smelled muddy water.

"You have cast aside the glorious raiment sewn for you," replied Arim Ben Ymir. "You have not eaten of the feast the Lord prepared. You have dwelt in darkness and seen where darkness has come for you." His voice was raised as if addressing a crowd. Perhaps he was, Leitus thought. But there was no response. The sound rebounded from what had to be the walls of buildings. "The hollow face has opened its mouth and you will all be swallowed therein!"

"You bring no news," said Leitus.

SUBIUS AND THE OTHERS

Inside the inn the public room was dim. His daughter, Sidar, wearing a soft, white robe, barefoot, was drying her long, dark hair with a pale cloth. Daylight filtered through the shuttered windows. The girl smiled, a little unsure, but he knew her mother had already explained some of it. And then he understood that was probably why she'd let him wait outside.

"But why now," he started to say, "why not last time when—"

"Why did you give up?"

"What?"

"Last time," she said. "Sidar, this is Subius, your father. Say hello."

"Give up? Give up?"

"Hello, my father," the young girl said. She kept rubbing the towel behind her head, smiling at him.

"She seems to have good teeth," he said.

Sira raised one eyebrow. "Are you buying a goat?" she wondered.

"Hello, Daughter," he said. He shifted from one foot to another. Took a deep breath. Looked at the sturdy thirteen-year-old with wonder. His daughter. He didn't really feel uneasy. Just that he thought he should feel uneasy. He actually was unaccountably comfortable with all of this.

He stood there just staring.

Fortunate is the man who discovers that what he truly

wants and needs are the same thing instead of wailing regrets into the hollow face of death, he thought.

"Why don't you kiss her?" Sira asked, not untenderly. "It may be, my Roman, that we've become old enough to be a little young again."

He nodded, bending and lifting the almost plump girl into his massive arms. She was warm and smelled fresh, he thought, as a garden.

"Yes," he said, kissing her forehead. "Thank the gods."

Sira went into the adjoining room. Things bumped and scraped in there. A tinny clatter next. He wondered if she were preparing food.

Not a bad idea.

He set the child back down on her bare feet.

"Do you like living here?" he asked her.

She shrugged.

"I guess," she said. She tugged one long, lustrous strand of hair. It gleamed in the diffused, whitish daylight.

"Do you have many friends?"

Another shrug. "Sure," she told him.

"Would you like to visit Rome?"

And then Sira was in the doorway and he realized what she actually must have been doing besides talking to her daughter while he'd sat outside, because she was dragging two large, bound packs into the room.

"We're ready," she was saying, deadpan. "Would you like to eat before we go?"

So in under an hour they were out the door and she didn't bother to lock it.

"Why had you lingered here this long?" he asked her, heaving both bulky packs on the strap across his back. "Were you waiting for me?" He grinned.

They went out the archway into the over-hot street. The heat haze hadn't improved. The whitish buildings shimmered.

"Is that your best guess?" she asked him. "It seems others are waiting." She gestured with her head at the line of people blocking the street ahead.

"My popularity swells," he said, narrowing his eyes,

"like the Nile in flood." He pressed his delicate lips tight. "Stay close to me."

He recognized the soldier he'd knocked down. And three new faces that he hadn't. Some avid-looking citizens too.

"Should we try another street?" she wondered.

He shrugged.

"It's been my experience," he said, "that what you meet in Rome wearing robes, you meet in Gaul in cowskins." They reached the group, which made a semicircle around them. Sidar pressed close to her mother's legs. He stood there, the big packs humped up on his shoulders so that the sinking sun's angle cast his haze-blurry shadow over the man he'd laid to waste earlier. The soldier glared and aimed his spear with stiff fury.

"Now, scum," the fellow said in Egyptian, pressing his big lips together to help him feel fierce. "Now you—"

"Yes, yes," said the ex-gladiator, shaking his head, trying that language, "let Roman man me for to—"

"They understand Greek around here," Sira reminded him.

"Let us not quarrel," Subius said at once, in Greek. He'd learned that tongue in childhood before he was captured and brought to be a slave in a Roman province. "It is foolish to fight. I, too, have suffered at the hands of the Romans. My wife and child and I but wish to—"

"I have suffered at *your* hands, fat scum," said the soldier brandishing the spear.

"Let us be reasonable," Subius entreated.

"They seem unmoved by your eloquence," Sira remarked.

"As by my good looks as well," he reacted.

The spectators and semi-participants were offering scatters of advice in a number of dialects. Subius made ready to dump the bundles and draw the short sword he wore strapped straight down his wide back under the robes.

"Hear me, good people," Sira was trying, "let us

pass in peace. My husband and I—"

She was interrupted by a tall, bony priest in a red tunic with a black hood that hid his face in a pucker of cloth.

"Slay him," he commanded, as if with authority. "He has defiled the temple of Isis and means to give comfort to the enemies of our goddess!"

"Eh?" wondered Subius, who'd understood part of it.

"Slay him before he joins the others!" screeched the priest.

Then, before any could move, he leaped as if his legs were coiled springs, a dagger suddenly sparkling in his fist, ripping the blade at Subius' face even as the big man stepped back, shrugging the packs away and getting his blade free.

The priest's voice was a bellowing scream without words as he scrambled to attack again. The ex-gladiator blocked two wild cuts and thrust straight in so hard, the blade poked out the man's back and drove him three feet into the air. He hit the street. Dust puffed up and his legs thrashed in a spasm.

Subius regathered his bundles and went on, sword held ready.

While the rest were debating whether to try their luck, Subius and his family were almost through the group. Their backs were to the fallen priest, whose heart was spewing his life's last blood into the gutter, so Subius didn't understand why they were all suddenly falling back in shock and disarray. Little Sidar was screaming something, and by the time he turned the priest was charging again, hands clawing, daggerless this time, his punctured body emptying like a slashed wineskin.

Without dropping the packs, Subius slid to one side and slashed the skinny throat that was exposed as the black hood flopped open.

The nearly severed head bounced on the chest, the strange shout spraying horribly from the slash wound. One hand caught Subius' robe and locked as he backed away to let the body fall.

It didn't fall. A woman was screaming. Sira snatched up her child and ran clear as Subius tried to spin away. The bellowing, bleeding corpse whiplashed along with him, the hand gripping, the legs, impossibly, still supporting the ripped body. He chopped the hand away and kicked the rest across the street. It rolled and spattered blood on the building wall.

"Come," he told Sira, except she was ahead of him. When he glanced back, the ruined dead man had levered himself upright again and was staggering blindly around while whatever mad forces animated it spilled wildly out. And he remembered fifteen years or more ago in Caesar's camp in Britain (the rumor had run through the army and Leitus had eventually confirmed it) when a tribune had been chopped to pieces but refused to die, trying (for no apparent reason) to slay Leitus. The rumor was that devils were after the young Roman.

But why me? he thought. *Or is it what they all say when it happens?*

They ducked into a side alley.

"We're getting out of here," he said. "We're going to live in peace and comfort."

"Follow me," Sira said. "I know shortcuts to the river."

He'd sheathed the bloody sword without losing a step, and he still had her belongings. He was drawing heavy breaths by the time the mesh of lanes they'd been following had unwound into the main thoroughfare along the waterfront.

If, he reasoned, the butchered thing was still following, it had to be far behind. The idea that it might still be coming was not good to consider. If he had to, he could chop off all the limbs and let the torso wriggle along as best it might. The idea was almost amusing in a giddy way. Almost.

They paused to get their bearings. The water was smooth and the middle distance lost in haze.

"We're near," he told her.

"Mother," Sidar said, "why are we running? Who was that man?"

"The Romans are coming," Sira said with grim

understatement, "and people are not themselves."

Subius snorted.

"Woman," he said, "that's one way to put it."

"Why are the Romans coming?" his child asked him, this time.

"It would make my head spin," he replied, "to explain it."

They came around a bend near where Subius had left his ship. There was a small crowd gathered. A man was shouting, haranguing. He stood on the white stone steps that went up from the wharf.

As they hurried past Subius looked up. Odd sight, he thought. A blind man was standing with the speaker, tapping his staff on the steps, apparently trying to work his way down. The little dark man addressing the crowd was going strong, except no one there understood a word of Hebrew besides Subius, who knew only fragments.

Ben Ymir raised both fists to heaven and flailed the air. His beard flopped wildly. His words were like (Subius thought) thunder and darkness, a gathering storm spilling over the horizon. Or were they merely a madman's outcries at the demons that beset him?

Subius shrugged and dragged his steps, losing ground to Sira and Sidar. He was fascinated by the blind man tip-tapping down another step, angling toward the river, head tilted, haggard, sun-seared, barefoot, in tatters. He noticed the staff was a sheathed sword. That was interesting. Then he recognized the profile and was amazed.

"Wait," he called ahead to his family.

The sun was setting. His shadow stretched up the stairs. Leitus' shadow spilled over the building wall above. The Jew's penumbra seemed carved into the building itself as he hurled his message into the dying day, across the dimming water, into the silent desert beyond.

Subius came near the blind man.

"Leitus," he said. "Leitus Sixtus."

And then he realized there had to be some connection, that the murderous priest must have linked him somehow to Leitus.

What am I thinking? Am I a credulous old woman?

But he was nervous, and the idea haunted him now.

"Who is this?" asked Leitus, tilting his head.

Get on board, Subius thought, *and set the sail. . . . Get on board and set the sail. . . .*

"By the gods," he said, "it is you."

Arim Ben Ymir was still howling condemnations into the night.

I've discharged that debt, Subius thought. *No one can say I haven't discharged it.* He meant his vow to Spartacus when he'd sworn to defend his son Leitus. He'd certainly defended him. He'd nearly died several times doing it. So he really had no obligation left and he had a family to worry about now. It was a fact that Leitus drew disaster to him as if he were the center of a dark whirlpool. *No one can say I haven't discharged it. . . .*

"It is me," said Leitus. "That is my misfortune."

"Leitus, what has happened to you?"

Sira and Sidar looked anxiously up at him. The sun was cut in half by the far embankment. The deep red spattered the grayish-violet water surface.

"Subius. I am Subius."

Leitus groped and caught his arm. Gripped it.

"Is this a dream?"

"What happened to you?"

"Have you a year to listen?"

"Your eyes?"

"I got some sand in them."

Ben Ymir had just cried out as if to damn the dully flowing sun for going out as the earth swallowed it, shouting words that only Leitus would have understood if he'd been listening.

"You are doomed because you have made a dark garden in yourselves where the evil vines flourish. You have made your sins a wall to keep out the holy light! You are all eaters of blackness and the poison fruits of blackness!"

"Come with us," said Subius.

"I have to find my wife and my son."

"Laudable, but you lack means. Have you a son in truth?"

"Yes."

"I have a daughter." Subius liked saying it.

"I was to meet them at Gizah."

Subius led him now. They headed for the wharf. His ship was moored there, phantasmal in the elusive, fading illumination, so that instead of a block merchant craft it might have been a mythic ship set to cross the sea of dreams to some magical country. The point of a quest, Subius was to think years later, lay in the looking alone. The gold you finally got your hands on had no magic. But the gold of dreams, ah, there was coin to buy eternity.

There was a sudden high, shrill scream of pain and fear. Subius looked back at the steps where Ben Ymir had been. He strained to focus. The sun was just dull color now; the pale buildings and steps were just a glimmer. So he never was certain, but it seemed that two or three abnormally tall figures were standing around the fallen speaker, who was a dim sprawl on the vague whiteness that twilight had flattened into a dimensionless wall.

The ex-gladiator felt a sinking chill in the pit of his belly.

The curse of Leitus, he thought.

He moved the Roman exile toward the gangway. He hoped his eyes were playing tricks, because he had a sick feeling that those tall lads were going to be coming to call shortly.

As he and his family and his blind friend clattered up the boards to the deck, he said:

"Leitus, there must be a prophecy that you will bring me to my doom no matter what I do."

"Where are we, Subius? By Jehova of the Jews, I cannot believe I have found you in this strange place!"

"I found you, I think."

"Where are we?"

"On board my ship." Subius turned to Sira. "Go

below with Sidar." He tossed their belongings to the desk. A few torches burned at the masts. "Who's on board?" he called across deck. A small seaman hopped down from a cabin roof. "Where's the captain?" Subius demanded.

"I have to find them," Leitus was saying. "Help me, Subius. By Jove's ears, I cannot believe this. . . . How are you come here?"

The young captain was on deck, wanting to know what was the commotion.

"Cast off at once!" ordered Subius. "For your lives!"

"What's this?" the captain asked.

"Heed me! I'll make all clear once we're safe."

If even a sea's width will be sufficient. . . .

He drew his blade and went to the gangplank. Kicked it loose. It fell and clattered on the stone quay.

"Cast off, then," said the captain.

"Make haste, I tell you!" Subius reinforced, staring hard to see who might be coming. He thought he saw the tall shapes at the end of the wharf. "Make haste, damn you!"

FLACCHUS

Starless night was solid at the tall windows as if the chamber had been sealed. The huge grated door at the entrance was shut. Naked slave boys with torches stood around the inner walls of the forum. The light flickered over the crowded floor and seats.

Flacchus sat on a gilt, cushioned chair in the center of the room. He was fat as ever and more flabby than before. Naked. The black stone rested in his lap. He faced the seats where more than a quorum was present, as he'd thought at one point earlier, giggling softly, moistly.

The seats were filled: in the first row in senatorial robes, purple-trimmed, a dozen pigs were tied upright, squirming and struggling, oinking miserably; behind them a row of goats in togas, horned heads tilting morosely; then sheep, frantic and bleating.

Around his chair, half a hundred actual senators writhed in a heap. He'd commanded it, and under the sway of the black stone, all obeyed. They crawled, circled his seat in a fleshy mass, some in despair, others with frantic, furious faces . . . around and around . . . and, at his whim, the stone forced them into particular acts of degradation.

He held the stone up to eye level in both hands in a squared-off gesture reminiscent of Egyptian wall carvings.

"Speak to me," he crooned, while the bodies sweated and groaned and sloshed together around him. "Show me what to do." And the memories, madnesses, forces, stirred in the stone and echoed in the swirling of his haunted brain. *Lead me to the others!* It swirled, and Flacchus was a chip spinning on the flood again. *Lead us, carry us all to the place of merging!* Because they were incomplete and they knew it now and felt it now and no amount of entertainment could assuage the need to merge with all the others and become the total, dense mass that was legion, the uncountable minds and souls racked with the longings of millennia. . . .

It spoke. And he knew what he had to do. He saw it clearly.

He stood up and picked his way across the soiled bodies. He paused to look idly down at senator Trivian, former master of men and power in the city, paused to enjoy the man's misery. A tall, knock-kneed, elderly senator stood up at Flacchus' unspoken command and emptied his bladder over Trivian's face.

"I shall keep you for my toilet," Flacchus said. And then went on out of the Senate, several slaves, on cue, falling in step behind him, holding their torches as in a sacred procession.

He was carried back to the villa in a closed sedan chair. He kept one naked young boy in there to while away the time spent traveling.

By the time they reached the gate and were turning in past the cracked and headless statues, he had pressed the boy down flat on his face on the cushions and was rocking the compartment as he worked his jiggly, massive hams and hooked himself into his agonized, helpless victim, who could barely breathe under the sweaty weight.

Snarling, gritting his teeth as he rolled massively to his passion's peak, he thought thoughts and saw sights that defied description and chewed on needs with no names.

With casual ease his puffy hand found the boy's

throat and closed fiercely, yet without heat, as he ripped to a deep, muffled burst, luxuriating in the final contractions of panic and strangulation.

Feeling refreshed, he climbed out, seated himself on a burly slave's naked back, and kicked him into a rapid crawl up the steps and into the dark corridors of the sprawling, mainly deserted place. He was preoccupied and only distantly enjoyed the sobs of pain and dismay as the man's knees tore and bruised and left a bloody trail on the tile. He was thinking about the world he planned to carve into shape once the last stone was his. Because no one knew he'd found the second one in the chamber under the villa.

He and the myriads within him had magnificent plans that would dim the passing sports and minor pleasures he'd been forced to satisfy himself with.

The slave buckled and collapsed by the time he'd crawled halfway down the spiral stairs to the underground river. So Flacchus walked the rest of the way to the bottom. Then he stood by the water rush in total blackness.

He could see quite well, he discovered. Some of the former possessors of the powerglobe had senses that would have been utterly blinded by the weakest ray of daylight. A degree of those senses were his now. He was dreadfully enhanced as well as multiplied.

The water boomed past, flowing from hundreds of miles away, starting under Britain and ending, deeper and deeper, somewhere in the unknown continents to the far south. The semi-composite minds generally agreed that it emptied into a lightless sea where dread creatures from the lost past, all teeth and terror, swam and ripped one another, and anything unlucky enough to come there, with cold fury.

The water was flowing the wrong way for where he meant to go, if it had mattered, which it didn't. Because Flacchus gripped the stone as if he meant to throw it and pressed it firmly between his buttocks, rammed it in hard and felt the first chill bubble of superhuman energy glow up into him. The force lifted him slightly.

A flabby tic of a smile creased his face as the power pried at him. His body loosened. Became like a dark cloud. He filled his mind with a vivid image of where he meant to go. The world was loosening as the force bubbled up. The only solid thing was the speck of denseness at the heart of the sphere, the secret, suspended fragment of substance from the heart of the earth. The world was bending around it. Distance and time were bending and now had no more meaning than in a dream.

"Now," he or it said, "I step through."

Then his mouth repeated the statement in the form:

"G'naaluupppsss'gnaadraata."

And he stepped into the landscape that hung like a shimmering tapestry in the darkness over the black river.

It was like walking into a waterfall that slammed into him and swept him instantly away. A giddy sensation. A whizzing as the scenes melted into one another. . . .

IN THE PYRAMID

Morga took the black globe from under her robe and held it with casual power. Bita winced, feeling the strength of the thing. In this case, there was no swarm of shrieking desires and torments as with Flacchus' crystal. This sphere had been dominated by a single will of superhuman vitality and subtle perception—a being who had perished ages ago.

Bita sensed that this stone had subtly enfolded the young girl as in a cloud of black mistiness, a cloud that blurred places in her mind, blending her desires with its own and filling empty places in her undeveloped soul.

The girl poured her will through it as though through an amplifying lens.

"Obey," she commanded, and this time the tall creature stopped dead at her word and the other came out of the archway. Both raised their clawed hands outward, palms up, and dropped to one knee. "Bring my brother and his mother."

The two things moved, awkwardly, rapidly, limp-bounding, seemingly eager to obey now.

Bita collected what force she had, made a fist of it, and struck at the wiry thing that stooped over her son. She hit squarely and felt it stagger as if the invisible beam of will were a solid shaft.

"Run, Artur," she yelled.

Futile. Antony whacked at the one who had already

snatched Bita from her feet. The blade skidded as if hitting a stone carving. Almost broke his wrist.

"Gods!" he cried.

Arturus cut from the other side without better result and then the claws had him.

The girl had lightly leaped down into the corridor.

"Bring them along," she said. She tucked the black stone somewhere under her silky black robe and walked briskly ahead, ignoring the frustrated, amazed, and scared Roman, who shrugged, then went for her, since all else had failed, thinking he'd hold the blade to her neck and see what came of it.

Very little. Just as he reached her, a black wall fell on him. When he came to himself, he was out in the desert under the risen moon, flat on his back, numb.

Nothing hurt, but he felt weak and distant. There was no memory after he reached for her. He assumed he'd been struck on the skull, but there was no lump or pain.

He sat up. It was as if he'd simply slept. He could see the silver sheen on the Nile.

He was out of it and knew it. He'd been simply brushed aside. He sighed. It was the end now. He nodded. Accepted it. He'd been brushed aside in so many ways.

Too bad I let the goddess down, he thought. *If there was one. . . .*

It never occurred to him that he'd actually done what was needed. He'd brought them all together through the storm.

Later Bita was to understand that she and her son had to be taken by Morga because there would have been no other way to penetrate the inner circle of their enemies. There was no help anymore from outside. What light there was glowed now only within human beings. It was up to them to fan each flicker into flame. Abram had told her that at the last feast of Passover. He'd called her outside while a lesser priest was reciting prayers. They'd stood on the porchlike structure that leaned against the side of his family's house overlooking Jerusalem. The last violet-reds of sunset were draining away. The city was a hush of pale buildings and soft touches of flamelight as the candles and lamps were lit inside the windows.

"Tonight we eat bitter herbs," he said to her, holding one supporting post as if it were a staff.

"Yes," she said.

"We should eat them every day."

"What can people do? They try."

He almost laughed.

"Hardly, young woman," he said. "They barely try." His face was long, detail-less against the darkening western sky. "All men live on the surface of the greatest wonder, and in fear and ignorance they decorate the surface until they can no longer see inside at all. Do you understand?" She nodded. "What fools they are. When Moses pointed to the Promised Land and said he could not enter therein, they believed the Promised Land was a place in this world and so they believed they had reached it."

"Decorate the surface," she said, thoughtfully.

"With ritual and vain imaginings. False gods or false ideas about true gods. And false ideas about the Oneness. Most of all false ideas about the Oneness."

"The god with no name."

"God cannot be named. That is the secret. It was not forbidden to say, but there simply are no words for Him, no way to express Him that is not a lie." Abram's voice was vibrant. "The clumsy fingers of the mind can never close around the Oneness."

"The light too bright to look at."

"The light without shadow or source. This is a world of clocks and measuring rods and the light cannot be measured. The light is in all things, even the wicked, but is not seen." He was speaking, she thought, to himself now. "The burning bush will be seen again, but this time in man, a beacon of holy fire. He will shine so brightly that even the blind will praise His Glory."

"I think that once I was touched by the light," she murmured.

"Yes. But you walked with the *Elohim,* the gods, and

they cannot come here anymore. Expect no aid from without, Daughter not-of-my-blood. The *Elohim* left a spark in you of their special brightness. Not the Unnameable's radiance naturally, which even gods are helpless to capture or pass to another."

"But—"

"You will have to leave here soon, Daughter not-of-my-blood. The power you have been given must suffice you and must grow greater."

The horizon above the city was dark now. The soft flamelights seemed altered reflections of the hard, uncompromising purity of the stars.

The priest inside was still chanting, fluid, monotonous.

She'd sighed. Didn't quite believe it yet. He might be mistaken. Why couldn't he be mistaken?

ON BOARD

At dawn they were moving out into the reach, crossing the last arm of the bay as they edged into the Mediterranean.

Subius stood on the bridge deck, staring at the line of darker water where a muddy river spilled out into the sea. Leitus sat on the deck, back resting on the rail, inflamed eyes squeezed shut.

Subius was watching a dark, wavering blur at the riverhead about three or four miles astern. A ship. Coming on a slight angle to their course.

He frowned. Turned to Leitus. "How are your eyes now?" he asked.

The younger man made a slight sound of disgust and unease. "They hurt," he said.

"Open them."

Leitus shook his head. "No," he said. "Where are we?"

"Off the coast."

"I have to find them."

"You'll have to open your eyes sooner or later."

Subius squinted at the ship. Big, square, black sails tilting. Moving very fast. Glanced up at the mast where their own canvas seemed fairly slack. The crew below deck (not slaves, since Subius would have none) were keeping a good rhythm at the oars.

"I should throw myself overboard," Leitus said.

"What use will I be now?" His head lolled on the wood.

"Thank the gods you still live," said Subius. "You always complained too much." *But stood like a man when backed to the wall, I admit.*

The young captain stood by the tiller. Called over:

"Master Subius, do we set course for home?"

"No," he called back, still watching. "It's up to you, Leitus."

Sidar had come out of the cabin and was standing near them, barefoot, big-eyed, curious.

"Is he blind, Father?" she asked.

Leitus twisted his face into a nervous smile. "For a long time," he answered her.

"What is it like?" she wanted to know. "Is it dark?"

"He was not always like this," her father told her. "This is my daughter, Sidar," he told Leitus, with almost sheepish pride.

"Greetings," said Leitus.

"But why did you say you were always blind?" she persisted.

He sighed. "I never saw what to do with my life," he said. "Life was like a blackness to me. Nothing at either end but black walls, and nothing behind those walls but nothing." He rubbed his face.

"I don't understand," she said. She was looking now where her father was looking. The black ship was going to intersect their course as it passed them.

"That is called bitterness," Subius said.

"Men like to dream that there is something behind those walls," Leitus said. Bit his lip. "But there is nothing." He twisted his mouth. "I knew a Jew who saw the horror of emptiness, and it made him mad."

"Well, that craft there is not imagined," Subius changed the subject. "A long, swift ship it is." He tapped his fingers on the rail. *A strange ship. . . .*

Leitus was listening to the waves bumping and breaking along the hull. The pain in his eyes was duller. He felt sick in an unexpected way. Had no appetite at all. Kept dozing off. Sleep was good because there were pictures to look at, movement and color, and things that made no sense, made sense.

But just then, half asleep, there were the tall terrors leaping out of the sand-cyclone at him. He was fighting back as the grating stuff rasped his sight away. He started awake, heart racing.

Monsters in the desert, he thought. *Was that supposed to mean something? What mockery . . . what a world . . . lying, cheating, sickness, death, madness, brutal rulers, cruel lawkeepers, religious maniacs . . . children born dead or killing their mothers to be born . . . the pleasure of the arena. . . . the poor, the crippled, the slaves, and all the sick satisfactions of the rich. . . . Ah, and I was in the desert and monsters clawed at me . . . and they were nothing to the monsters of hypocrisy and lies and smug ignorance. Those are the real monsters who can never be defeated because men will never really face death. They'd rather invent infinite ways to take their minds off the nothingness that waits for all. . . .*

He sighed. Tried to doze again. Felt the sun where it rose higher now than the rail, pressing warmly at his face and setting a yellow glow behind his eyelids. It occurred to him that he was thinking strangely because he couldn't see. He felt trapped in his skull. He'd often had similar reactions moments before falling asleep.

The body quickly starts to fail . . . gets damaged . . . the mind weakens. . . . He slammed his head back hard against the wood. Saw spots. *Stop thinking,* he thought.

The ship tipped and tilted him down into another scene: a clear stream this time, water flowing under full trees that sifted the sunlight down into exquisitely bright flecks and spatters. Mysterious chiaroscuro currents stirring beneath the surface. His own face was reflected there, faintly outlined beside slender, delicate Bita. It was a memory, more or less, of the time they'd been escaping from Rome while she was pregnant with Arturus. They'd paused by the stream to drink. In the water they were shaped on the flowing glow and subtle shadows so that their outlines held the changing stream within them, golden stipples sparkling where their hearts would be. . . .

His head banged the board again. He felt it. He could

think almost as if awake. But, perhaps because he couldn't open his eyes, the memory stayed vivid, soundless: just the two of them touching, overlapping, reflected together, sharing the same greenish-gold flowing texture, the same sheen of sunbrightness.

What is this? he was thinking as the supernally beautiful, mysterious water rippled through their fused images. *Why must I see this?*

He struggled to wake fully. There was something. Something like weeping and swelling joy and something that seemed to pour through him like a tremendous current washing away his fears and thoughts, brushing his struggling mind aside with impersonal yet infinitely tender strength.

His mind flailed but found no grip . . . just the pure, perfect brightness . . . and then a bass sound he didn't know was a voice yet, much less Subius' voice, was shaking the glow until the image broke and he was left with just the dull red in his eyes and a shock of longing so strong that he cried out.

"Get up, Leitus," the voice said.

Leitus grunted. Rubbed his face. Didn't dare touch his eyes yet. The red was like a soft wall across his face.

"What do you want?"

"There's a boat crossing our prow," the ex-gladiator said.

Leitus cocked his head as if to listen to the scene. Spray ticked against his face. The waves slip-slapped the hull over the steady rush of the bow.

"Fascinating information," he reacted.

"There's a woman bound to one of the masts. And what looks like a boy bound to the other."

"A woman and a boy?"

"I think so. They could be the ones you seek, but I haven't seen her in so long. And we're not that close to them."

Leitus got up. Supported himself on the rail. Tilted his face into the wet, steady wind.

"Can we get closer?" he wanted to know.

"Impossible. She's too quick. Best open your eyes, if you can."

Leitus swayed there. Felt the deck tip, the railing thump into his hip. Chewed his lower lip. Clapped one hand across his face. Sighed. Strained. The lids stuck, hurt. There were scabs. He felt them open as if the skin was being freed by needle tips.

"Ahaaahh," he uttered. Dug his fingers and thumbs into his temples.

The eyes came open, sticky and agonizing. He paused in the windrush and spray. Then clawed his hand away as if it were being pressed over his face.

"Well?" wondered Subius. He squinted, not quite focusing on Leitus' hurts. He saw the creases of fresh blood. His belly nerves clenched.

Leitus faced the same reddish wall, slightly brighter because his face was in the sun and the lids were parted. Not even a blurring, just a blankness of heated flesh-color.

He slammed his hand back over his face and groaned.

"Not good," Subius said, looking away at the black ship now crossing in front of them. "Not good at all."

"Father," said Sidar, looking back toward the mouth of the river, pointing. "Look there."

A wedge of dark clouds was pouring down impossibly fast. The brilliance of the morning dimmed. The clouds looked almost solid. They were already cutting off the rising sun.

It's like a river of heavy smoke, he thought. It seemed to be funneled down the riverbed as if in dark, mirrored amplification of the waterflow. Subius estimated it at about three miles across and four or five miles high.

"I've got a bad feeling about this," he said. "Go below," he told Sidar. "Stay with your mother."

Leitus had sunk back to the deck. The worst was the worst. He wanted to doze again. Drop out of the world.

"Is it she?" he asked, because that was all he had left to focus on besides the reddishness walling him into himself. "Subius, is it she?" It was focus or scream.

I'll just rest, he told himself. *Then I'll do something . . . then . . .*

The strange jet-black vessel moved quickly out ahead of them. The square sails were trimmed blood red.

Subius made out no crew on the deck, just the woman and the boy bound to the two masts, facing one another. He made out some winged creature carved near the stern. The masts bent as the sails elbowed the ship into the wind.

"I cannot tell, Leitus. We'll try and follow. There's something unnatural here," said Subius, glancing back at the long storm mass that was pouring directly across the sea toward them as if in conscious pursuit.

CLEOPATRA

Naiar stood on deck, yelling at the sailors who hadn't yet deserted. Behind him part of the city lay under a haze of smoke. The Romans were burning the western quarter, it looked like. People were fleeing to the sea in panic now, jamming small boats, overturning rafts, sitting on logs and planks, swimming for ships.

"Cast off, you dogs!" he yelled. No response. "Cast off by the queen's command!"

"There's not enough of us," someone called back. "We couldn't pull half a league."

"Fools," he raved, rushing down the planking and bending his back beside the black man, fumbling with the oversize ropes.

He was calmly desperate now. He kept telling himself that once they were afloat, he'd give her the drug. She would forget everything and he'd teach her, raise her like a child until she knew enough to love him again. Yes. The sea would carry them to safety. There were enough men to steer, and if he had to do it alone, he would.

He went, frantic but controlled, from massive cleat to cleat, fingers rasped bloody until all the lines were cast off and trailed in the water.

The current was already taking the huge craft. The wood creaked terrifically as it scraped free of the pilings.

He stood panting, swaying, then plunged up the planks, straight up, as if he'd rehearsed it, because they fell behind him just as he bounded onto the deck. The other crew were already diving over the rail. The wiry, expressionless black slave stood on the pier watching, silent, as the golden floating palace slowly moved out into the current, smoke gathering over the city as the on-shore winds unfolded it. People were still fleeing to the water.

Antony had staggered to a city gate. The main force of Romans had entered already. He'd seen one of their encampments in the fields on his way in. He watched the smoke draughting down to blanket the pale buildings.

A dozen guards leaning and standing at the gate studied him laconically as he wobbled up, blasted by the heat and the unreeled miles behind him. He was sore, dusty, and probably twenty pounds thinner than when he'd set out to battle Octavian mere months ago.

"An officer," he heard one say to another.

"Where's he been," another wondered, "wrestling crocodiles?"

I'll fight as many as I have to, but I'll see her before I die. There's no question of that.

He was afraid now of the blank wall of death in front of him. The utter silence. The fact that whatever they'd done, said, or been would be over and he would never see, touch, or speak with her again. Whatever they'd done together would be buried in blankness without appeal.

They were, they cared, struggled, hoped, dreamed, discovered tenderness and passion and regretted all the rest. And everything would sink into nothingness forever behind the bricks of time. A hopeless, cold terror fingered his heart.

I'll fight until I see her. . . .

That was important. To end with her so that would be the last thing. The last. He would have begged for more hours or days had there been anything to beg it from.

Antony marched straight through the gate, past the soldiers. He didn't look up. A voice was asking him something. He finally listened.

". . . Which legion, sir?"

"What?" he said, not looking, the soldier keeping partial pace with him as he entered the city.

"Which legion are you looking for, sir?"

"I have to go to the palace." He paused and looked around. "I'm a general, as you see."

They didn't. But he could have been. His specific insignia was torn away.

"But, sir—"

"I need a horse," Antony commanded, inspired by the idea. "I'm late."

"No doubt," someone muttered.

"A horse," he repeated.

"What is your name, sir?" asked the polite soldier. He was tall and patient. A shadowy figure to Antony.

"Marcus Antonius," he told them. He put one hand on his sword hilt and waited in the smoke-stained sunlight, eyes hard, dark points in his wasted face. His brassy, battered armor glinted dimly under layers of dirt and dust. They might have laughed at him but didn't.

"Ah," the foot soldier said, comprehensively.

"Get me a horse." Then he saw one, tethered to the wheel of a merchant's cart—a spraddle-legged, bony-barrelled old mare. "A fitting final mount."

"Is it he?" a high-pitched voice asked behind him. He didn't turn.

"If you go in," the soldier said, gesturing so that another freed the mount and led it to the fallen conqueror, "you won't be let out again."

Antony levered himself up onto the beast's back. His left side hurt and his neck was out. He felt miserable. He chuckled.

"Just where," he wanted to know, "would I be going?" He took up the reins. "If you want to fight, I'll fight."

"We have orders to let you alone, sir."

"How generous of my frog-faced brother-in-law."

Octavian knows he doesn't have to kill me; he merely has to wait until I find someone to hold the sword at the right angle so I won't have to keep trying.

And he kicked the hesitant animal into the city. The serrated back jarred him as the small hooves banged and slipped on the smooth street stones.

Octavius Caesar was at the palace at the moment maddened Naiar cast off the ponderous barge.

The Roman dictator was slim, dour, and nervous. He stood in an open, floor-length window that overlooked the harbor and watched the royal barge ponderously slide along the wharf.

He wrinkled his nose at the first curls of smoke from the inner city.

"Bid them extinguish the fires," he said to the generals at his back. "Have they found him yet?"

"No," said one, "he must have fled."

"Don't touch him when you find him."

"He's fled," the same voice said.

"No," said the commander. "He'll come here. To find her."

Octavian was actually watching, though he was too far away to recognize him, as Antony rode the awkward mare down the stairs right to the water's edge.

Antony yelled up at Naiar, who had paused at the rail to make sure the ship slipped clear.

The bony horse kept pace at a half-walk. The sun was going dim as the smoke settled down over the city. It glittered pure gold and blue where the reach opened to the sea. Here the colors had gone lurid.

"Is she on board?" Antony shouted, except he knew she had to be because he'd seen the barge moving from the palace gate and recognized Naiar and knew the priest would have to be as near to her lap as he could crawl.

"Go away, you son-of-a-bitch!" the bald young Egyptian yelled back. "How dare you still live?"

"Live? Do I seem to live?" Antony returned.

"You destroyed her, you son-of-a-bitch!"

The Roman kicked the poor beast into a poor gallop, reining it in a semicircle, then angling for the edge of the long pier. He stood up on the stirrupless saddle.

There was never a better rider in Rome, he thought as he used the momentum to leap out and up. He sailed, sank, and just managed to catch his strong hands on the nearest oar hole. Slammed his breath out against the side, then crawled into the rank dimness of the galley-slave deck.

"I'm coming, my love," he muttered. "I'll be with you straight." *We'll be together. . . . They won't be able to say we weren't together. . . .*

The blankness was there again as he blundered through the hold. It was closing down, the vast, senseless darkness grinding over him, a mountain of stone.

Naiar raced across the smooth, deserted deck, knowing it was already too late, because he couldn't have both cast off and watched her. He fled down the hatchway, slamming into Cleopatra's quarters, where the girl slave still crouched. Her face was turned to the bulkhead wall now, forehead resting on the dark, polished wood as if in ritual despair. So he actually didn't have to cross the long cabin to prove just how late he was because he could already see she was still in the oversize chair behind the burnished table, tilted back as if pinned by the masses of gold she'd draped herself in. Her breasts were bare this time, ample, soft, still firm and fairly small.

So he stopped and stood. Swayed. The details didn't matter: not the tiny squeezes of blood across the nipples or the dull mist in the half-opened eyes.

Naiar stood there and was still standing when Antony burst in. The wall of darkness was closing down behind him, so that if he took even one backward step, he'd be crushed. And then Antony wasn't moving because the table hit him across the hips. The falling wall stayed suspended while he swayed, panted, and looked at her face. Nodded several times.

The only thing now is to sleep, his brain told him. *There's nothing I can bear to remember so I have to sleep.*

He drew his sword and held the handle out to the young priest who blinked at the gesture.

"There's no time to find a Roman," Antony said, "much less a friend." His eyes stayed on her face. It was all there, and nothing too. All that had gone before, and nothing. "You'll do. Take it." He waited while the priest stared dully, hands shaking slightly. "You don't have to stick it in; just hold it steady."

FLACCHUS

The landscape was running colors, pale grayish-green and melted lead hues. It was like swimming up out of the water, except there was no water, just the dark tunnel opening and the streaming tones resolving into a misty landscape of soft hills and dark trees.

Flacchus found himself on a rutted road soft from rain but no longer muddy. The sky was tin-gray. The road cut into a wide, flattened-down valley with green, forested hills shaped like mounds. The way ran directly to the biggest hill in view, rimmed by pines and oaks, about a mile from where he stood.

He could make out the massive stone blocks that made a circle on top like, one of his minds thought, the foundation for the Tower of Babel. He could no longer have been sure which mind was his or another's. He was the swarming thoughts and urges in the stone. He vaguely recalled the actual entering when he'd lain on the rock bank of the underground river and felt the terrible pressure pushing into his skull, seeming to split the forehead itself and squeeze into the panicked, bubbling brain. . . .

He thought about when the three stones would be joined in him and fuse into one. He smiled, waddling with his fat-man's walk down the slope toward the Roman encampment he knew was just screened by the wall of trees at the foot of the big hill. As if they'd been waiting for him.

The air was damp. The mist lay close to the grass and summer brush. He and they were pleased. The thoughts were pleased as they considered the trap they'd set for the girl.

He paused a moment. Took out his stone. Kissed it. Murmured to it, calling now to Morga's stone, as he'd done before. When he spoke, the trapped minds wrote red words on the surface of that other sphere. Sometimes he spoke to it when she was aware and could reply, which was how they'd agreed to meet there in that special place at a special time. Sometimes he spoke to it when she was asleep or distracted and she never knew because her stone (she sensed this only vaguely) had its own purposes and made its own pacts.

"We are here now," he crooned to the ball of blackness. "We await you."

Because, he thought in the churning plurality that had become his mind, *she will come here hoping to trap us. . . .* The Flacchus thing grinned. Sighed with excitement. Licked the dark smoothness as if it were sugary.

Because she couldn't have guessed his real advantage. Even her powerstone couldn't know it, not until it was too late to save her. He'd made his invitation one moon cycle ago. Planted the seed and now was about to harvest the crop. He grinned and sighed.

She didn't answer this call because she was clinging to the rail as the storm whirled her ship toward destruction. But her sphere heard and understood.

We will meet, it replied, *and join our power.*

The point was, he'd found the second one himself. Under the villa, in the chamber where a shaft opened to the sky hundreds of feet above and where another seemed to have been sealed up in the floor directly underneath. He'd found it lumped under a rotting garment that softly tore to shreds when he poked at the bones underneath. The yellowed skull had fallen so that the jaw had nearly engorged the dense ball of jet.

He was smiling and they within were pleased as he waddled on again, bulbs of flesh jiggling, up to the open gate of the wooden palisade. There were sentries posted outside. Inside, cooking fires were already started and men were washing, relaxed, working on their weapons and gear.

"Excellent," their mouth said, smiling, taking the jet ball out and tossing it up and down on one cupped palm like a child might.

"Hey, there, bellyful," called a guard derisively. "Are you come to juggle for us here?"

"Entertainment," somebody else said.

Another:

"He looks right for you, Validius. He looks like his ass is soft as lard lumps."

Much laughter. Flacchus cocked an invisibly plural eye at the glossy globe. "Juggle," Flacchus said, nodding. "Excellent."

The first to speak was already beginning to bounce up and down in place. His puzzlement as his accouterments began to jiggle was already changing to fear as the second to speak now found himself twitching into the air and slamming back down hard on his heels.

"Oh, excellent," said multiple Flacchus. "After we juggle for a time," he told the commander, a stumpy, short-bearded man who'd come close enough to listen just as the third sentry was in full motion, "and enjoy the juggling, why, then we'll form up our nice men and stroll up to the top of the hill, where I'll ask you to construct another fortified camp." He sniggered. Kept tossing the stone up and down.

The commander's eyes were a black glitter of fury. His jaw clenched. He cleared his throat.

"You men," he snarled, "stand still! You retarded gnats! Are you all mad?" Glared at Flacchus-the-many-in-one. "How did a civilian like you get out here? Have you bewitched my men?"

Flacchus held an incongruously and unpleasantly thin finger up to his lips.

"Shhh," he hissed. "Now *do* be nice, Milles Gloriosus," he simpered. "You'll build the camp and do every little thing I ask and just *see* if I'm not sweeter to you than ever your mother, the famous whore, was."

And there, they within him merrily thought, *we'll wait for shrewd little Morga the witch to bring our missing parts to us. . . .*

ON BOARD THE BLACK SHIP

As the black ship sliced steadily ahead of Subius' broad-beamed three-decker, Morga came from below, her silky black robe flapping and snapping in the freshening wind.

She stood between the two masts. Bita was bound to one, Arturus to the other.

Bita was trying to remember a detail from their escape from the pyramid. Morga had led them through a long tunnel that debouched downriver where the black ship had been moored. When she'd looked back, the storm over the desert had seemed to funnel down into the earth. Or was it an illusion?

Bita had been unable to resist. The dreamstone's power had gripped her as if in bonds of black iron.

"I need you both," Morga told them. "I've tied you for your own protection. It would be foolish for you to wander about this vessel and meet the crew."

How true, Bita thought. She was facing the stern and could see what manner of creature was braced into the tiller.

"I would be more content," Arturus said, "back in Jerusalem."

"In the hands of my dear father?" Morga wondered, stepping closer to him. He looked at her levelly, coolly. She knew he wasn't afraid. He interested her, suddenly, in a way she wasn't prepared for.

"How am I your brother, then? I know my father and love him."

"Leitus," she said.

"None other. So you know him too? Is this spying or more witchcraft?"

"Well," she murmured over the spray rush and thrumming of the sails, "you don't know *my* mother. Your aunt." Turned to Bita lashed to the other mast. "Your sister."

Bita took it in. Remembered.

"My sister?" Some piece of an old vision flickered in her memory.

"When Leitus was in Britain he met my mother."

The vision of Leitus in a moonlit field, lying athwart a naked girl. A vaguely familiar girl, except that her face was mostly hidden by his head. A battlefield, dead men lying scattered in the phantasmally moon-brightened fog. . . .

"So you say that my husband," Bita worked it out, "was your father by my sister?"

Morga nodded.

"This is a family reunion," Morga said. Half smiled. Her look was bitter. "And then there's the Black One. The Lord Aataatana. They taught me he entered my mother too. They taught me that, and what would such knowing make me but what I am?" She wasn't even half smiling this time. "An abominable creature." She shrugged because, Bita saw, she'd accepted that. Swallowed it like poison and kept it down where it had eaten her slowly, eaten her childhood and soft hopes. "But I am powerful because his black, cold spew filled her womb with his foul might."

"You believe this?" Bita asked. Not that it couldn't have happened, she understood, but because it would be better to believe it had not.

"I feel it," said the adolescent with ancient eyes.

Bita, because she was facing sternward, first saw the storm. It was coming at impossible speed. Boiling, black and green, lightning walking, flicking all around as the sides reached out over the sea, she thought, like wings. And she felt the first shocks of the black beams of unlight again, the incomprehensible senses of Aataatana. She felt the weight of the dense mass at the heart of the contorted winds, the mass Ata somehow rode and sheltered within.

"Look there," she said. It already covered half of the sky. The sun was lost. The black edges seemed to flap for the horizons.

Morga turned, snarling and surprised. It was the same unnatural fury that had trapped them in the pyramid. She whipped her left hand from under her robe. The other ship falling back in their wake, she noted in passing, was a pale chip in the gaping embrace of smashing wind and cloud.

She held the black globe close to her face. Bita tried to see clearly but the radiations from the storm center were weakening her again. She was fading in and out. The wild clouds seemed to whip across her mind and leave inky stains.

Morga stared into the gleaming sphere that went hollow when she unfocused and opaque when she tried to fix her stare. In the hollowness she saw what she'd expected: thin, long red letters formed and strung into sentences. The trapped personalities in that gem were dominated, unlike Flacchus' stones, by that single, ancient consciousness. It had worked carefully to gradually take over the girl. It fed her myths and lies and part truths with a pattern. Much later Bita was to partly comprehend what Abram would have known at once: that the dreamstone was itself being manipulated from outside or deeper within.

You told me I was safe, Morga accused silently.

Which mortal is ever safe? Fear not.

"Will I survive this?" she whispered.

The spidery, crimson script wrote:

He does mean to destroy you.

"Can you touch his mind and purpose?"

We know him.

"Will I be given power over the stones?"

You will be given what you can bear.

Morga was fifteen, but no fool. "Some truth," she murmured, "some lies."

What do you ask?

"Do you tell me everything you know?"

Have you lived forever?

"The devils betrayed me," she complained, meaning the tall, black creatures.

They are also his children.

"Can I trust anyone or anything—even you?"

Trust completely what you control completely.

She put the globe away, hating herself a little for using it. Meanwhile the storm was over them. She gripped the railing. The other craft vanished in the waves and smoky clouds.

"Cut me free," demanded Arturus. "Give me a chance to help."

"You are safer where you are. We shall not be destroyed."

And then the corkscrewing sea and air hit them, shuddered them, snatched away the sail like a magic trick, heeled the ship insanely into a wall of foam and swept them into a vast, accelerating circling.

Bita and her son had glimpses of the other ship as the sea reeled around them, half crushed and spinning like a chip.

Morga crouched and held on with both hands. The tall being at the tiller stayed at its post as the wind and sea swirled them faster and faster. The masts went except for the shattered stubs holding the prisoners. The sweep snapped away from the steersman's clawed hands.

Centrifugal force shoved Morga against the rail so that she couldn't spin overboard. The tall demon had another fate: a gust took him, snapped open his leathery wings and spun him up into the churning chaos.

Arturus felt like the ropes were slicing him into sections. Spray hit so hard it stunned and welted him. They spun even faster. Finally it sucked away all his consciousness. His mother had long since passed out from the sheer proximity of the dark, fuming power at the violence's center.

ON THE COAST

Leitus and Subius were still on deck. No one else, including the captain, was left on the mastless hulk. Sidar and her mother were below. Through the haze of his flickering consciousness, Subius kept desperately wanting to crawl down to them, but the spinning force kept him pinned beside Leitus on the wildly tilted deck.

Leitus had given up. Since no human voice could have overcome the windsound, he had no idea what was going on. He suspected he was dead and in the process of being swept down to the underworld to face the judge of souls.

Somewhere along the way his awareness drained into night and he believed he was addressing Charon on the dread ferry over the lightless river Lethe, the somber shore of forgetfulness looming gradually closer:

"Hear me," he was telling the stooped giant who leaned on the tiller that steered the long boat strewn with swollen-looking flowers. "Hear me, O Charon, why did I live? A man's senses are like bottomless holes or sucking quicksand in a slimy bog. Each sense craves and yet can never be filled. The eyes seek sight after sight, the ear to hear what pleases it, the nose attractive scents, the hands to glut themselves on carnal touches. I was no more than a machine devised of tormented wishes." The ship glided nearer the far shore. "Even when I was fed and sated by sex and had gold and food enough, I was still nothing but a sack of blood and excrement. O Lord Charon, there was nothing, nothing, that did not fade or turn to dust."

And then the long, somber barge touched the silent shore and the black fogs of forgetfulness closed around him and there was nothing more. . . .

Until he woke in a grinding, roaring, heaving, splintering crash. Things hit him in the body. Then he was underwater, then up, choking, blowing air, spinning, then scrambling on solid shore. He staggered, went to his knees, then up again, tottering, falling finally on a stony beach. The ship and the storm were gone.

When he put his hand across his eyes and took it away, there was very little change in the dimness, so he knew it was almost evening. He'd discovered he could tell the time of day, to some extent, that way.

Voices. He wasn't alone. Subius and his family. Down the beach. He could hear the crumbling, soft shatter of the surf.

"Here," he cried out as he groped, tripped over what had to be a broken beam from the ship. Fell and got up. He was getting accustomed to that. "Subius!"

"Yes," the ex-gladiator called over.

Leitus blinked hard. His eyes didn't hurt anymore. They remained blank except suddenly there was that perfect sheen of waterlight, the golden glitter of his and Bita's overlapping reflections. The memory that wasn't quite memory.

If only it could always have been like that, he thought.

And for an instant there was only the reflected light vivid in his mind, and it was as if he slept wide awake . . . all senses blanked and there was only the coruscating, vibrant golden fire. . . . And then his eyes were open and he could see the coast and sea. It was late afternoon. Thick trees grew close to the water. Low, undulant hills swept smoothly down to the beach. He saw Subius and his family wading to shore, the shattered ship beyond, bundles of fabric opened (when the hold cracked apart) and streaming out on the choppy water like strange banners. And everything tinted soft and subtle gold so that green was not green, neither blue, blue, but all tones of a sourceless golden glowing that was nothing like sunlight. In fact, when he looked at the sun directly, he saw a soft disc. It was as if his very eyesight lit what it looked at.

Incredible, his mind said.

Subius and his family seemed to flare and spill beams of soft light so that he was barely aware of their physical bodies. He felt strangely giddy and almost peaceful, as if all the storm and terror had never been. Eager, too, like a young child; eager for nothing in particular. Just for being alive. . . .

"Ah," he voiced, in a kind of ecstasy, "so wonderful. . . ."

Because nothing else mattered, neither what had driven him here nor what he had to do about it, as if time ran somewhere else, far away, and couldn't touch the shining wonder that absorbed him. He felt that if he remained absorbed nothing would ever touch him. Time would run, yes, the shadowy body would shrivel and die yet the shining wonder would endure forever.

He walked, wrapped in the eternal and the ordinary, over to Subius, who was holding his child in his arms and didn't realize what was different at first, but then said:

"Your sight has been restored?" Then he looked back at the choppy water where the wreckage bumped and scraped.

Leitus was thinking about the phenomenon, trying to find words for the perfect symmetry that was all but consuming him.

His effort made it flicker. The brilliance stuttered like suddenly frail and wounded wings. Opaque flickers and then the gold was gone.

He groped. Pressed his eyes. Felt heavy. His head hurt. His body was all soreness from the pounding he'd just taken. He strained to see again, to call back the image of the shimmering water, but his thoughts strained and rippled the hushed surface.

He clenched his fists and snarled.

Just as the storm came smashing into the rough coastline, the black ship falling to pieces, decks flying up, mast stumps pulling loose, sides crumpling and splintering on a low wall of jagged rock—just then Morga finally worked her way around against the pressure that held her pressed down flat.

Her arm was freed and she was able to get the powerstone where she could see it, the centrifugally amplified mass pressing into her thin chest.

Do I live through this? she wanted to know at the first impact.

Fight him, the stone wrote in itself.

She tried. Braced herself, poured her entire will into the globe and said a tremendous NO to Aataatana, who she knew in his semi-real form was riding in the dense eye of that unnatural cyclone that spun them in foaming orbit.

She strained and kept fighting.

"Free me!" she cried. "Free me!"

As if in answer, the wild water slammed over her and swept the two captives into surf.

The rest of the vessel went down almost at once, so whatever or whoever had been below decks was lost.

Morga was rolled safely up onto the pebbly beach. She sat up in the spent flex of breakers, cradling the dark ball like an infant at the breast.

"I won," she was saying. "I won."

She stood up. Looked around at the misty, jagged coast.

I may be close to home, she thought.

Inland, dense pine stands gave on rich green fields and smooth hills in the bluish distance.

The storm seemed to have collapsed in on itself and recoiled back out to sea.

Bita and Arturus stood watching it. He was shrugging off the loose ropes. His mother was already free.

Morga waited for them. She looked into the black

crystal. She hadn't asked yet but it was already spelling out:

Take them toward the sunset.

"Where are we?"

At the water's edge.

She raised one fine, dark eyebrow. She was drained and suddenly hungry. People were always trying to rule the body but, she reflected, the body always won, sooner or later.

"Which water's edge?" she asked.

Where you now stand.

She frowned. She sensed something was wrong. The stone had recently been evasive in its replies.

"Damn you," she murmured, as if it were a person.

Bita and Arturus came up to her. She was slightly unsure of herself, looking at his eyes. A miracle they were alive. Yet she needed them. There was more proof of purpose in her life. The cold power of the stone was filling her again. She sighed and drank it in. Licked her fine lips.

His eyes were a rich, dark blue. She kept looking at them. She thought he showed a faintly hopeful expression.

Well, why not be hopeful, she thought, *he's had a life, a mother and father to love him. . . .*

She looked away and actually held back tears. "Come along," she told them, "unless you're hurt too badly to walk."

Bita just watched and waited. Rubbed her cramped arms and rope burns. She remembered seeing the other two stones in the hands of the priests long dead in that underground chamber when Iro had tried to sacrifice her to the lord of the underworld.

She sensed the strange consciousness the crystal contained. Sensed how the girl, for all her personal energy and strength, was a thrall to it. Abram had known about these things. He'd told her they were called the dreamstones by the Hebrews because they magnified the user's dreams until the images became more substantial than the solid world.

Bita knew she could not overcome this girl. Not yet. Her sister's child. Was that true? Why would the girl lie?

But by Leitus? she asked herself. *How dreadful. . . .* Her son's sister, steeped in darkness. *Yet perhaps she can be reached. . . .*

Morga had decided to worry later about the unsettling answers the globe had been giving her.

Can my dear father in hell have something to do with that? she thought.

"Follow me," she said, turning her back, uncomfortable looking at Arturus. She felt faintly ashamed and almost shy. It irritated her. But the feeling was as real as the tears had just been. She bit her lip hard. She never had cried. Never. "Otherwise . . ." she trailed off. She was shy of saying that, too, and any threat seemed pale and meaningless. She vaguely wanted to drop everything and simply be friends. But she never actually put it to herself that way. She never had friends or loves or family.

They went inland up the damp, grassy slope as grayish clouds pulled apart like cotton balls and the sun came out, setting, in their faces, dark, clotted red above the softly gray-green hills.

They passed through long shadows and high, saw-edged weeds with tiny violet flowers in netted brush.

A lovely place, Bita thought.

"Where are we going?" Arturus asked. He was contemplating overpowering the frail-looking girl whose slim body showed in the unrent but saturated robes. They all were still squishing as they walked, but the air blowing down from the hills was sweet and quite warm.

Morga glanced into the sphere again, moving her lips silently to ask:

"Should I . . . should I be . . . friends with them?" Meaning him. And she knew that too. Meaning him.

Don't fear to lose him, it told her. *Feel your body quickening with desire for his body. Think of both your bodies naked together.*

She covered the stone with her hands and blushed.

But even if he'd been beside her and could have seen her face, the blood hue of the failing sun had painted over it too thick to show.

But the seed was in soil and she knew it. She pressed her lips together.

"Where are we going?" Arturus repeated. "Mother, must we follow her?"

"Listen," Morga said, not looking back, "I have things I must do. It is too late for me to go another way."

"Why not try one?" Bita suggested, thinking that if they were truly deserted by the gods and alone in this world, then unless all beings helped one another there was no hope for anyone.

Morga kept her eyes straight ahead. The fat red sun was cut in half now by the horizon as if it were sinking behind a wall. Shadows pooled in the valley. Insects droned and scraped cries in the thickets. The earth was soft underfoot. The wind stayed mellow. She remembered that there would be no moon.

"Which?" Morga asked Bita. She was trying not to look at the dreamstone. She'd never realized how hard that could be or how much she'd come to depend on it.

"The one that leads away from the darkness," Bita said.

Morga smiled in a kind of wince.

"How are you so sure of yourself?" she wondered. "I am living my fate. What has been forced on me. I didn't choose it." She was looking at the stone now. "I know nothing more." She sniffed and shook her head. "The Jews—do you hold their doctrine?"

"Which doctrine?" Arturus was interested. In fact, he was the one who'd actually studied.

"The invisible goodness," said Morga.

Arturus' eyes went distant as he prepared himself for a good discourse. He was trying to think of how a rabbi might get into the subject.

"It is not invisible," said Bita, "if you have eyes to see with."

Arturus moved up beside her. Morga glanced at the

red fire scribbling in the sphere.

What is best for me to do? she was asking silently.

The redness wrote:

Take your pleasure. Nothing exists that you cannot see or feel with your powers. All they want is to possess your powers for themselves.

Yes, that made sense. The priests, warriors, everyone she'd ever known, proved that proposition.

Arturus was saying:

"Let me ask you a better question. Why would you want to consort with devils?"

"Devils?" she responded, not quite looking at him. She was keeping her focus away from the stone again. As they walked the subtleties of twilight gradually absorbed them.

"Yes. And magic. All forbidden things."

"Who forbade them?"

"The Lord God."

She was smiling.

"Which one?"

The sun is down, so there's no sense trying to follow it farther, she reasoned. She wanted to spend some time with Arturus. There were new things here to be considered.

A dense grove of twisted yew trees was bunched in a gentle crease between two low hilllocks. A tiny stream worked its way downslope in snakelike loops and swirls.

She stopped, and they sat down there under the thick branches. The running water bubbled and hissed.

"I have learned," Arturus was saying, "that there is only one God."

She settled her back against a tree trunk. Her clothes were nearly dry. She thought about getting a drink from the stream. Knew there was some dried meat in her belt-pouch. Wasn't really hungry yet. The first, soft-looking stars showed above the hill not like the keen points of the desert sky.

We have come very far, Bita thought.

"By whom," Morga asked, "was this wisdom imparted?"

"Abram the Wise. And others." He pursed his lips, trying to see her features in the failing light. "Are you really my sister?"

She had the globe in her lap. She slipped off her sandals and stretched her long feet.

I think we're in Britain, Bita was thinking. She sat cross-legged and watchful, treating Morga with the deference she'd show a momentarily sedate wild creature.

"What does it matter?" Morga reacted. "We don't know one another. It's just words to us."

Put the woman to sleep, wrote the dreamstone. Morga couldn't stop herself from reading it though she still feared it saying embarrassing things again. *Then take your pleasure naked with this boy. Your body wants him. You are afraid yet you want to touch his naked parts and to be so touched in turn.*

"Yes," she murmured. She didn't blush this time. The globe rested where her long thighs joined her groin. Her hand, unconsciously, had been jiggling it for a few moments now. It was like a strange, new hunger, she thought. It had always felt tingly and pleasant to touch herself there, but this was deeper and almost ached. She admitted to herself that she really wanted to touch him.

"Yes, what?" he wondered. He was sitting, facing her, a depthless outline against the faint, dark fire beyond the hills. The air was a hush of warm, sweet odors. She felt soothed and excited and, for the first time, as if she were part of the soft earth and the grayed tones of gathering evening.

Is there truth in what he tells me? she asked. *Is there one God with power over all others?*

Why should a Jew be right more than another?

Yes, she agreed.

"Why do you believe what the Jews tell you?" she asked him. She kept moving the stone, each slight friction a surprise and amplification. It was getting hard to think about anything else.

"Because Abram was wise," he answered.

"How do you know that," she returned, "unless you are wise yourself. Are you wise?"

She watched him, his subtle outline. Then she concentrated on Bita because the need was rushing forward now, carrying her into the sweet and lustrous darkness. She pushed her will gently through the black lens and wordlessly said *sleep* to her.

Then we'll be alone, she thought.

Yes, said the dreamstone.

"Why do you listen to that," he said to her, because he'd just figured out that she was consulting the thing. Abram had warned him about that too: "The Devil," he said, "had balls fashioned in Hell that he gives to his favorites to steal their souls with poison truths."

"It is wiser than your Abram," she told him. "And it gives me power. Power I've seen, not something invisible." Her hand hesitated a moment, broke rhythm. "Not the mouthings of little toad Jews, who are not the only ones to talk as they do, by the way."

Teach him, the stone wrote, *and learn pleasure yourself.*

"I don't want power, as far as I know," he said, thoughtfully. He turned and looked at his mother, who was stretched out on the sweet grass, breathing deeply.

"She's sleeping," Morga said.

"I'm weary myself," he said, "and hungry and thirsty too. We might have all been drowned dead in the sea." He sighed. "Yet, it is all passing exciting. There's so . . . so much to life that I feel yet have not yet known. I sometimes fear I'll die too soon." He stared at the stars. "I feel I have some great thing to do in this world." Shrugged. "I'm afraid I'll die too soon." Nodded. She was just watching him now, listening. "I don't know . . . the Jews are wise, but they keep indoors too much for me. . . . I miss my father too. Do you know where he is? Can your ball of wisdom tell you?"

"Yes." She started the rhythm again. It was a desperate itch. "Anyway, maybe you won't die so soon."

"Will you help me, then?"

She shrugged. Her fingers stroked the cool, hard ball over her mound again. More need had gathered itself in the pause.

"Mn," she murmured. "I don't know yet."

"You're not so terrible as you like to seem." He shifted closer to her. Her face was faint paleness above the dark garment. She'd tugged it up, he'd just realized, and her legs were bare. "Where are your devils now?" he wondered. "Did they drown or sink back to Hell?"

Her scent was very nice, he thought.

"I'm not terrible at all," she said. "But I am hard to deceive." The ember between her legs was flaring into deep fire now. "I know things."

"What things?" he wasn't quite mocking. He was still thinking about the creatures, thin and deadly. He liked her scent. Spicy, he thought. He was resisting an impulse to run his hands over her long legs from bare toes to the top. He was surprised and interested by his reactions.

"I could share my power with you," she suggested. "And no harm would come to your mother." That surprised her. Because she meant it. She strangely wanted to give him things. Please him. There was no reason for it, she noted.

He seemed to accept it, though his mouth doubted: "Why would you do that?"

"Why should I lie? I'll have power over you but there's no reason to hurt you with it."

The rhythm was now virtually ecstasy. She felt the need was sweeping her along like a river rushing downhill toward a waterfall. She sensed the drop ahead with eagerness and fear, greedy to fall. She didn't feel awkward in the least, suddenly.

"Are you really my sister?" he wanted to know.

"We have the same father, so they say."

"Who?"

"Those who told me."

He smirked. "Your ball there?"

She held it up to her face. Her body seemed to keep the movement without it now.

"Is he my half brother?" she asked playfully.

He is your husband, it said.

She put it beside her, at arm's length, her fingers

lightly touching the smooth, heatless surface. It felt so good to touch.

"What did it tell you?" he asked, not quite mocking.

"It said it makes no difference," she told him.

She raised one leg and pressed the soft, perfectly formed foot firmly on his chest. His hand instantly covered it. Gently. With wonder.

"Arturus," she said.

"Yes?"

"Come to me."

She felt him hesitate. But she didn't want to force him. She kept her eyes away from the globe. Kept squeezing one thigh against the other. It was exquisite. So she didn't read the red script that now was writing:

Make him worship you; make him kiss your feet and every naked part you have; teach him pleasure with the lash; make him a slave; teach him the exquisite way.

She deftly hooked her heel around his neck and tilted him onto her. As she floated down to the inner falls she was able to take time to say:

"They told me you were a great warrior."

He was moving to get up. Her hands now held him behind the neck. He noticed the sphere spilling its unread messages in what he didn't recognize as language yet.

"I've fought no battles," he said. "I did well enough recently, but I haven't proved much yet." He nodded, thoughtful. "Who said that about me?" Her scent had him giddy now. He felt the hard swelling between his legs and wanted to touch it—no, wanted her to touch it. Their faces were close. Her breath held a new scent that he wanted to cover with his mouth and inhale, consume.

"I want to share with you," she told him softly. *This was not what I was intended to do, but I no longer care what was intended by anyone,* she thought. "All that matters is being strong and taking whatever you desire."

I was kept from this too, she thought, *but now I know and I will have everything, even things no one else has ever thought to want. . . .*

Because she believed she'd found the cure for the icy deadness in herself. The blankness of the past.

"But I was taught," he started to say.

"By Jews?"

"I was taught that all we possess is on loan from God."

"An invisible god who can offer only invisible rewards." She bussed his lips, her thighs squeezing her groin against one of his legs now. "I am a goddess and will make you divine yourself. Then it will no longer be on loan."

She tugged his face close, touched between his legs, and the force of nature did the rest. He almost sobbed with need, trying to taste it fully, to lap it from her lips and breathe it from her body and grasp it in his questing, stunned hands. Her breath hissed softly through her nose as they prolonged the kiss and his hands drifted over her bare legs and up above.

Neither noticed the stone reeling off a seemingly unending flow of advice and comment, commands and philosophies, as if a stream of articulate blood spilled through the crystal depths.

Meanwhile, Bita lay in deep, relaxed sleep. She'd discovered, however, that Morga's magnified will had no power over her inner consciousness, the subtle light that glowed when the outer senses were extinguished.

In a blurry way she saw what was happening with her son and Morga. Dreamseeing, in colors like an unvarying predawn gray.

She noted living things around her in the woods and bushes. Small scurriers and snakes. Nesting birds. Hunting owls. She saw them as pulsing gushes of life-energy flickering among the living patterns of flowers, trees, grasses.

Her attention was really on the dreamstone. Her mind was trying to enter it past the spilling red words. She felt the twisted, powerful minds that had been prisoned there, the stiff, violent movements of the dominant personality who'd actually molded Morga. She had a dreamlike image of this one: a stunted, lumpy, semi-human shape that suggested a bipedal reptile.

She grasped that Morga was being deceived and led to a purpose not her own. Perhaps not even the thing in the stone's purpose either. She groped for the underplan. Pried into the stone, letting herself fall into that dark miniature universe, aware of a gathering of some kind, a council of black, glossy, winged beings that were like insectile reptiles, clustered around a massive stonelike table where a molten spot flamed dully and highlighted their faces with red reflections. The biggest one, the master, wings partly opened, dominated the meeting. She could feel the gloating, the devious calculations . . . something to do with a ceremony on the surface world . . . a dark swirl reaching from far below to catch their victims . . . but who? Where? Because suddenly she felt panic at the wordless feeling that they were going to reach up and snatch her son away. He was fifteen now. In the month of the Lion. Fifteen. The prophecy had said fifteen. . . .

The stars had half wheeled down the sky by the time Arturus came back to the swish and whisper of ordinary time. He lay beside her in spent wonder and engorgement. The air was cool and pleasant.

He stared up through the dense leaves at snips and flicks of starlight. He was still stunned by what had just happened. Right after the brief pain when she recoiled on herself and tried to thrash free of him, the experience had been incredible. The squeezing heat, his desperate strokes, the almost agony that became a slow, exquisite sweetness and falling into fear and then past fear, rubbing himself over her, sucking at her spicy flesh, the pleasure coming thick and slow and startling and then familiar. . . . Just thinking about it now drew his hand back to his groin to feel himself stirring again. He wanted more, he realized. More . . .

He heard her slow and even breathing. Thought she might be asleep. Wanted to wake her and do it again now. Wanted it to last longer. He turned and looked at her slender but fully curved body, a faint shape in the filtered starlight. Rested his hand on her leg, softly followed the incurve of belly, hoping she would stir toward him. His other hand felt himself and the syrupy gathering of pleasure. He wanted it again. Wanted it always. Wanted it to last longer and longer.

The stone lay beside her, dark now. He considered doing it again even if she stayed asleep. Amazing how her body was such a package of delight! Mouth and groin . . .

And then she sat up, no, crouched to her haunches like a cat. She'd snatched up the sphere as if she meant to throw it.

"Come no closer," she said.

"What?" he wondered. A strange change of attitude, he decided. And then realized there were small figures all around them. *They must have crept like shadows,* he thought. His mother still slept, he noted. Heard her regular breathing. He debated whether to wake her.

"Do we fight?" he asked Morga.

One of the figures advanced a half step, silent. A weapon glinted. Said words that meant nothing to him. And she answered in kind and a dialogue followed.

Natives, he reasoned, which meant she knew where they were.

She pulled her robes closed, still crouching. "They were looking for me, my love," she told him. "They are my loyal subjects. So long as I am stronger than they are."

He stood up. He now was aware of hundreds more of them on the slope and probably in the valley too. Amazing so many had moved so quietly.

"Subjects," he said. "Are you a queen here?"

She touched him tenderly on his cheek with the hand that wasn't holding the dreamstone. Traced the line of his lips.

"More than any queen you've ever heard tales of, my love," she said. She felt tender and confident. She felt matured. The soreness inside her groin's parted lips was almost a pleasant memory now. "I've decided that you'll rule beside me."

"You've decided. Rule what?"

"This kingdom. And then as many more as we please." She leaned up and kissed him. "My love." She liked saying that. She wished that everyone would go away for a little while so she could sit alone and think about Arturus. And then savor all the more when she could touch him again.

His mother was awake now. She came closer. She was trying to remember and sort out what she'd seen inside the stone. It was desperately important to get an idea of how they were going to snatch her son.

"How will you gain these kingdoms?" she asked Morga.

Morga glanced into the sphere. It was still dark.

What now? she asked.

The red runes wrote:

March to victory. What you seek is waiting. You are nearer the end than you yet know.

"You will see how it is done," she replied to Bita.

"I . . ." Arturus began, uneasy.

Should we escape if we can? Bita was asking herself and feeling, somehow, no. She sensed they were here for a good reason and probably could not escape in any case.

"You love my son?" she asked. "Your brother."

They were all already walking, the smallish men that she realized were Pict warriors moving around them in supernatural silence. The air was misty and heavy.

Arturus felt a strange sense of mission and meaning. This girl had suddenly exploded his life and he felt tremendously energized. Imagined sweeping events, great clashes of arms, high purpose, charging on a wave of armor, bright steel and snapping banners, flinging into glory.

And he wanted her. To push that ecstatic greediness into her again, to let her draw at him, drain him until the emptiness erupted with astounding pleasure. He kept going over it and wanting it. As if the stone were already touching him, too, he imagined things he'd never conceived before: not just her mouth on him but her legs and wrists bound in chains with a beast's collar around her neck that he gripped while forcing himself deeper into her face, pulsing with almost frightening pleasure, working her long tongue over all the naked places down there. . . . Yes, after the battles and triumphs, coming back to her or taking her on the field among the dead and dying . . . and he next imagined how sweet it might be to press her flat on her belly and take her from behind. . . .

Ah, I love these things, he thought.

Do I love him? Morga asked the stone.

He gives you pleasure. Enjoy him.

Because he'd exploded her life too. She kept picturing things she wanted to do with him once the battle was done and she had both stones in her possession. She wanted to feed him sweets by perfumed pools and do all the forbidden things together. Because nothing could be forbidden her now. She was a goddess. She felt like a goddess. She would create a world for them both and swim in delight and play. . . .

"Yes," she told Bita finally, "I love him."

"We must first defeat the Roman tyrants," Arturus was saying. He'd come back to not thinking just about sex. He was contemplating returning to Jerusalem at the head of a liberating army. His ideas seemed to have no bounds. "Our power may undo many wrongs."

It's really my power, she thought, but laid a finger on his lips as they moved downslope through the wet mists and cool night, and said:

"Together we will change many things in the world."

ARIM BEN YMIR

He'd been raging against the darkness as the sun set across the bay and the giant, misshapen ones dressed like lepers or the dead had pounced down the steps toward the waterfront, brushing him aside so that he sprawled down the stone edges and hurt his bones.

The tall, oddly limping things went toward the water. He sensed they were not actually crippled as he understood the term, but rather unadapted to walk like men. Arim Ben Ymir perceived them as devils fledged from Satan's smoking nest, who existed only by drinking the cloudy sinfulness and ignorance of mortals. They were distillations of all that was foul in mankind. The enemy's children. And each one of them destroyed, he now believed, would free exactly ten thousand humans in hell.

So he followed them, saving his voice now for the confrontation when God would give him the power to smite them like David at the giant. Biblical tales spun in his brain. And where they fit events, there was purpose for a moment, reinforcing him with almost poetic ecstasy.

So he chased them among bales and packing crates, seamen and shadows, out onto the wharf and then lost them. But that didn't matter, because he saw the vessel sliding away from dockside and he was already smiling, thinking how foolishly they sought to escape Jehova's wrath in that cursed ship even as he unhesitatingly plunged straight into the water and sputtered up and, as if long practiced, grasped the massive rudder.

Ben Ymir smiled with smug satisfaction. Who could escape the arm of the Lord? He felt the holy land supporting him as he climbed to the first level and entered in the rudderslot, levered himself over and then dropped into blackness. Hit hard. Rolled so that his brain was full of whirling, flashing sights, reddish, purple, and electric green. He lay in the foul bilge water on hard, uneven beams and raptly watched the colors where God was writing his intimate message and even after the impact effect faded away he kept replaying the memory in awed peace.

And he knew what it meant even when the darkness began to reel around him later. The hull rolled and scraped his flesh raw. But he knew. And was comforted though all the great powers of darkness now sought his doom. He spun and tossed as they attacked that cursed ship. Rolled and battered he laughed, knowing that he could not be destroyed and that he would come to smite the chief enemy with the perfect word which would be given him. The message that would undo hell and free . . . he groped for the number . . . yes, free exactly 999,999 souls, all the souls trapped in the infernal regions.

"I have been swallowed," he cried out in strange joy, "like Jonah." The ship crashed and twisted insanely. It was Subius' boat and the terrible gale was slamming it to pieces. Scrape, roll. "In the . . ." Pound. ". . . belly of night . . ." Crunch, spin. "But when my sins . . ." Heave. ". . . are purged, I . . ." Roll. ". . . I shall be set free. . . ."

And now the flashing colors from the battering impacts were almost continuous, and Arim Ben Ymir swam in blessing as his head cracked into the sides or chunked on a beam in the spray of rapidly deepening bilge water.

When he was left sprawling in the sand by the withdrawn tide he could hardly have been told from the other wreckage. Except the message was there when he awoke, as clear as when he'd been hammered senseless in the shattering hold of Subius' ship.

He knew what must be done. He crawled to his feet and stumbled inland to do it. The Lord would guide his steps and arm him for the coming battle and sacrifice. Amen.

THE BATTLE

Subius led the way with Sidar behind him. Leitus was using the sheathed sword as a cane, less depressed now because, however strangely and briefly, the blindness had somehow lifted once and might again.

"This country feels familiar," Subius said.

Sira peered around uncomfortably.

"Is this Italy, Father?" Sidar asked.

"No, child," he responded. "I don't think so."

"I thought we were going to die," she said.

"It was the favor of the gods," her mother said.

They'd slept in a stand of pines on the soft, fallen needles in the sweet, rich air. Subius was sure there were no pines like these except in the northern mountains.

Naturally enough he'd led them inland in the morning. They'd need food and shelter.

"That unnatural storm," he said, "blew us farther than seems possible. We may be in Hispania, for all I know." He tried to remember if there were pine trees in Spain. His geographic notions were hazy.

"Where are we going now?" Sidar asked.

"Madrid, maybe," said Sira, without much confidence.

"I'm hungry," Sidar said.

"We'll soon find folk. This is a lush-looking countryside." *Reminds me of British Gaul here,* he thought, without even bothering to add how absurd the idea was.

Leitus was getting ready to try and see again. Ready to open his eyes.

Subius knelt and poked the loamy ground.

"Here's a sign," he said. "Lots of feet. Some bare." *Could be a small army on the march,* he added silently.

They went on. Over a rise into a dell. The tracks increased, if anything. No campfires yet. No discards visible. That surprised him. Any large group on the march, even the best-disciplined legions, tossed things aside: food fragments, bits of gear, broken buckles. . . .

Now they were in a valley following a well-marked road. The sun was behind them, waking fire on the hilltops, burning off the scarves and strands of fog.

Something flashed in the first sunbeams. Bright gold. Subius stooped. A chain and brooch. The brooch was a beautifully worked rune.

He studied it as they followed the thin road that had been overrun with footprints.

"What is it, Father?" Sidar asked.

"Jewelry," said her mother. "Very fine work." She took it from him.

"It's a neck chain," said the young girl.

Her mother gave it to her. "Some women would kill for the like," Sira said.

"What's this part?" Sidar asked, studying the pendant. "It looks like a funny letter."

Leitus thought about that.

"What kind of letter?"

"I don't know," she said. "Funny."

He pictured Bita's brooch. Pictured Bita. Remembered again bending over the stream in the spots of pure sun-dazzle.

"It looks like an arrow," Subius said. "No, more a harpoon like fishers use."

They were just topping a rise and could see across the green, sunny valley; the glitter of a small river winding partly around a long, low hill that dominated the horizon. The mists seemed to have gathered thickly over the crest. Down in the valley he could see hundreds of men marching. Made out weapons, horned helmets. No horses or war machines. Not Romans.

Leitus paused, clutched the sheathed sword, blinking rapidly as a few spatters of gold blaze took fire in his eyes and he glimpsed the chain Sidar was just clipping closed around her neck.

He knew it at once:

"That's my wife's!" he exclaimed. "She must be near at hand."

Subius turned.

"You can see again?" he asked.

"A little. At times. Strangely."

"You think your wife is here?" Sira asked. "But where is here?"

"She was in Egypt. . . ." Leitus shook his head. "I don't understand."

"I think I know where we are, but I don't believe it," Subius remarked. Because where the mist had pulled back he saw part of a circle of standing stones on the long, flattish-topped hill in front of them that walled off most of the valley.

Unless the British Gauls came south and brought their senseless stones and climate with them—though there's the rub because this weather is a little too decent to be British, he thought. But the air was somewhat thinner, somehow, and a little too cool to be Spain or any like place. *Whenever I'm with Leitus more than a one-half hour's stroke, disaster rises up and enchantments baffle the sensible course of nature. . . .*

"She must have been on that ship," Leitus said, the flickers of dazzle-light fading now almost like afterglow in the ordinary eye. He blinked his sore lids and hobbled forward behind the sheathed sword that he whacked and poked at the tread-softened earth.

"Easy," said Subius. "All these tracks are tending to the same spot, it seems."

I'll find a place to hide her and the child, he calculated. *Then I'll have a look up ahead. . . .*

The narrow road led straight to the central hill. Trees lined both sides as if it were a processional way. The fog still filled between the trunks here on the lowest ground, so that suddenly smallish men stepped, silent as shadows, from what seemed a soft, grayish wall without even having to level their spears or brandish the war axes and clubs.

Sidar moved close to her mother. Subius raised both eyebrows but hesitated to draw.

"What now?" Leitus asked, and paused with the scabbard groping in front of him.

"We're really in Britain," Subius said. "These are Northmen. Picts, they call them." Painted, dark hair twisted into greasy braids, set, expressionless faces. He'd fought some in the arena long ago. Quick, wild men, utterly fearless.

"Must we fight?" wondered Leitus. He prepared himself to strike at sounds unless the strange sight somehow returned at need.

"Little point. They haven't made a move and there are too many, if they do."

At least ten showing. One of them, streaked red and blue, shook his spear and pointed along the road.

Subius nodded.

They don't even have to disarm us, he thought.

"Come on," he said, "we seem to be going the same way."

FLACCHUS

He stood on the top of the limestone arch that crossed the circular stone pit like a narrow bridge. He looked around the perimeter of the hill. Under his direction, the Roman troops had built a palisade and were positioned for defense.

He grinned loosely and juggled the black stone from palm to palm. His filthy toga fluttered in the breeze. The sun was high on the morning side. He could see the Picts coming, fanning out off the road into the fields of undulant, long grasses.

As expected. As expected. He was quite pleased. Could feel the nearness of the other dreamstone. The stone in his hands actually felt it. The deep fires stirred within, the myriad fragmented personalities bubbled frantically. They all pictured or somehow conceived of the joining of the spheres into one dark dreaming, a transformation that would bring a new density to the earth. Matter, time, and space would reform around the single ruling stone and the laws of nature would darkly change.

The soldiers worked and waited with a comfortable impression that all was well. They believed they were simply doing a necessary job here under the lawful command of Octavian's chief general. Flacchus appeared perfectly reasonable to them. A stern, if somewhat stiff, hardworking commander in impeccable armor.

He danced with glee, watching Morga and her barbarians approach. They were gathering here by prearrangement, coming out of the hills, woods, and creases of the earth. Thousands concentrating on this spot, having moved up virtually undetected.

"She is very shrewd," he said. "She knew to bring an army." He—or rather, the plurality that was Flacchus—admired her and the intelligence that guided her even as he gloated over his coming triumph. Just getting her to come was a victory in itself. "Only a shrewd one would have been trapped, a fool would have lingered in safety." He nodded and smiled. "Once we are all joined and the cursed sun is dimmed. . . ." He glanced up at that blazing roundness and pictured it darkened by the thickened atmosphere into a permanent, reddish eclipse. "Then, then, we'll accomplish things and bend even the great lord Ata himself a little." Because then plural Flacchus would possess the central stone, the Black Grail, and all the energy that the maker had poured into it in times before time. "Don't fear, men," he giggled. "We soon fight for the greatness of Rome." A few of the war-tempered veterans saluted his words. The five guardsmen he'd posted around the opening stood still as granite statuary. It was nice mockery to talk to them since their minds were hollow until he chose to fill them. Flacchus peered down the pit. "It looks like a toilet hole, men," he commented. Spat into it. There was a steel ring set into the underside of the square arch with chains and leg irons attached. "We'll fill it with shit soon." He sniggered. Pressed the black, heatless sphere to his lips and sucked at it. They or he thought about things. About the black sun rising in a thickened sky. About pleasures no one could have described. . . .

Morga, with Arturus beside her, Bita behind, moved to the slope of the recently fortified hill. Her wild men had spread out into a great semi circle, partly enclosing the half of the hill they faced. The sun was bright and hot, passing noon. The mists had all burned away.

The fields, the slopes, were lushy green and the day's brightness seemed to gather in the trees and flowers.

How suspicious of him, Morga thought, *how distrustful. . . .*

One of the squat, fatless, lithe barbarians came over. A chief. Arturus was fascinated by his blue and red streaking, his greased, plaited hair. His dark eyes like small stones in a carven face.

"We did well to come prepared," she said to him, in his dialect.

He grunted. "Do we fight now?"

She was watching the globe.

Yes, it wrote, *the Roman has what is yours. Take it.*

"Yes," she said. It was all mixed in with wanting to be alone with Arturus; she kept thinking about that. The greatness and power was suddenly blurred a little.

"Some doubt you will keep your promises," the chief said, "once the fight is won."

He doubts, it wrote.

"You mean, Werri," she told him, "that you doubt."

"But then, others say, we are many, you are one." His face, eyes showed nothing. "But Werri tells them we have given our blood bond to her."

"Because we share the same blood."

He shrugged. "You are female," he said. "But we have given our bond."

She smiled. "Yet," she said, "you could not slay me, many as you are."

Another shrug. "Hard to explain men's blindness," he said, not quite expressionless this time, "yet there are those who even doubt that."

Attack, she read in the stone. *Kill him later.*

"All the land to the border will be ours," he reiterated.

"So I said. Now, attack!"

Several others were now turned looking back to the east above the channel they called the sea.

Morga glanced over. Another storm front was massing there. Moving fast. A greenish, dark stain on the cloudless blue, summery sky.

"What is this?" she asked.

Fear nothing, wrote the stone. *We must reunite ourselves with the rest of us. Call attack attack attack.*

She distrusted the strange arrangement she'd made with Flacchus when the stones had communicated. She feared treachery past her power to plan for. She'd expected the army, however, which was why she'd brought her own.

But now, another storm. That was no good. She squinted at it. What chance that it was natural? Very small, she decided.

Attack, repeated the crystal.

Does he love me? she suddenly asked in her mind.

Attack, it said.

As they went forward, she said to Arturus:

"Stay near me." She held the globe as if to throw it.

"Give me a sword," he said.

"You won't need one."

"Am I still a prisoner?"

"No. You know what you are now." She spoke to a Pict in dialect and asked for his long dagger, which he grimly handed over. "This will do," she told him. "You can slay me anytime you wish to."

"I have no wish to." Which was true. He just wanted to take all of her garments off and explore her with his hands and mouth and then push inside again into the incredible, thickening sweetness.

His mother watched him as he weighed the dagger and thrust it into his belt. She felt the crisis mounting. Felt the first, distant weakness as the storm reached from the horizon.

I'm not going to lose my boy, she was thinking. *Not if I can help it.*

In his fifteenth year, the gods had said, he would be lost to her. Not die, just be lost. She prayed now to whatever might be prayed to, to the vanished golden beings. *Just let me help him; just let me be lost in his stead.*

"Why are we fighting?" Arturus asked Morga.

"What we must have, my love, is in another's greedy hands. We must pry it free. And before my father does."

"Why must we have it?"

The Picts were trotting now, brandishing axes, clubs, blades, spears, beginning a rumbling, wordless, ululating war chant. The lead warriors were already on the slope and would reach the Roman wall in moments.

"With it we rule," she told him. She was excited. Leaned up and kissed him hard, too hard. He felt teeth under her lips. When he tried to hold her she pulled away, excited as the barbarians threw themselves at the palisade. "I'm through with my stupid life!" she cried. "Take them!" she yelled. "Take them!" Then, to him: "I love you."

The Picts were hacking at the wooden wall, others stooped with bent backs so that the rest could leap up and scramble over, screaming bloodlust, striking berserkly even as Roman arrows bristled in their bodies.

The first wave faltered. The second plunged in almost dancing with a kind of joy. Shouts. Impacts. Outcries. A mounting din.

The battle stirred Arturus' blood. He was afraid and yet was anxious to plunge into the madness, slash and hack, scream and claw. He suddenly had a sense that his destiny was upon him. Something tremendous waited for him. He felt it mounting from the pit of his stomach.

Strike, he thought. *Why not?*

Morga was ahead on the slope. The massed Picts were all committed to the fight now. The wooden wall had already gone down at one point.

"A breach!" she shouted into the din.

They headed for that point now, Bita behind, surrounded by a guard of about a dozen warriors. Morga held the dreamstone in both hands up to eye level and projected her will through it as if it were a magnifying lens. She paused on the level crest while the fighting boiled insanely around the breached section. The Roman defenders were now visible in the dust and crashing fury, their shields a solid square mass holding the Pict frenzy at bay.

Destroy, she thought.

Destroy, it wrote in red. Its darkness was now whirlpooling.

Like a solid shadow formed into a spear of force, she stabbed her magnified will through the crystal into the Roman shield wall.

Arturus was astounded: it was as if an invisible blade slashed a narrow cleft open with such violence that shields and men were sent spinning in the air. He glimpsed the dark beam slashing out as she strained, went pale, reeled with effort.

What a weapon, he thought. He wondered if he could wield it himself.

Through the dust he saw the massive stone pillars and the arch where someone who he assumed was the Roman commander stood overlooking the combat.

And then Morga was suddenly flung back and rebounded from him. He staggered and caught her. She desperately clutched the crystal globe with both hands. She shook all over, eyes rolling up into her head.

"Oh," she sobbed in a breath-struggle. "Oh."

He believed she'd been hit. Looked for a wound, in a kind of panic. The idea of that perfect slenderness torn appalled him. Found nothing. She went to her knees. The battle paused as if it were controlled by the respiration of a single warring beast, a single animus flowing through all the fragmentary, violent humans.

The Romans reformed their bronze wall of square shields. The barbarians regathered themselves. The man on the arch, Arturus thought, glancing above the ranks, seemed to be hopping or dancing on one foot. A big, round-looking man in a floppy toga.

Morga, Bita observed, was staring into her crystal sphere as she asked:

"What is this? Am I undone?"

And Bita saw the glowing scribble of response that seemed to be in Latin though she knew that was unlikely. Perhaps the words would be in any language you expected to see or in none at all, depending on your powers of mind.

Make peace, it wrote, *then strike again.*

Bita shut her eyes. She felt something stirring down under the hill. Something powerful but without a mind.

Leitus, Subius, and family had just come in sight of the hill. The impassive, silent barbarians walked them forward steadily.

"What's happening?" Leitus asked. He kept blinking and squinting. There were only scattered flashes of golden glint where he would see the landscape enhanced and smoothed over so that the stones on top of the hill seemed to shine as if the sun were rising there. The fighting men would be blurred together by the glow. The gold washed over the violence so that he could form no clear idea of what the vague movements he saw meant. Where men were stabbing and hacking each other to pieces he distinguished only flickers of life in golden sprays and auras.

Sidar was looking back the way they'd come. "It's going to rain again," she said.

The mass of steadily circling clouds was coming fast, covering most of the sky. The air was suddenly oppressive, static. The ground seemed to rumble deeply just below actual hearing.

"Praise Isis we're on land this time," Sira said. "I think we should have stayed in the city."

"That could be worse," reacted Subius.

"How?" she wondered, feeling worn and weary. Battered. "Birth with the head turned wrong, as it was," she said, "and giving suck, took less out of me than these hours with you."

"Tell me what's happening?" Leitus reiterated. "Is there indeed a hill full of men and brightness before us?"

"What's happening," said Sira of the stern mouth and grayed temples, "is that we have fallen from watery doom into the clutches of painted savages who may soon gnaw our bones."

"No, no," put in Subius, "these Picts are not cannibals."

"Ah," she came back, "you speak for them all."

"There's a battle going on," Subius said to Leitus. "Cannot you even hear the dinning?"

Because the clash and shouting was very clear now in the still air. Howls, impacts, and now a gathering, bass roar that put Subius in mind of some vast, uncanny beast. He turned and saw the dark, green-shot arms of the storm, taloned with lightnings and fanged with whirlwinds, reaching as if to rip the bright sun from the sky and swallow the green world itself.

Subius shook his round head and scratched his neck. An insect bite throbbed on the skin there, and his nails left a streak of blood.

The Picts guarding them grunted, poked spear butts into their backs. Kicked them into a trot. Several warriors were running ahead up the slope, eager for war. Subius supported Sira with one arm and Leitus with the other. He believed they'd be slain if they slowed too much. They hurried through the spume of their own road dust, panting in the afternoon heat as they hit the slope.

Down the gentle slopes into the far end of the valley, the first gusts came in shudders of sheeting wind. It caught him from behind and he was instantly running, floating on his feet, giving thanks to God whose hand he now felt comfortably holding him in the form of furious wind and cleansing rain.

Arim Ben Ymir's voice roared with the storm. He laughed and turned, danced, spun, fell on the loamy earth and rebounded to his feet, racing in staggers to the central hill that he hadn't actually been seeking any more than he was looking for anything except the continuing succession of miracles that was sustaining him.

He was ready to meet Satan now, filled with the glory of God. The hour was at hand.

"The time is here!" he cried. He laughed, fell, rolled, was kicked along by the wind down the last soft slope into the valley bottom. The storm loomed directly over him like an outcurving wall about to topple.

Arturus was stunned by the results of the fighting. It was one thing at a distance. He studied the paused battle: men lay twisting in pain across puddles of blood; a Pict stood holding his ripped entrails in both hands, looking baffled; a Roman with one arm sheared away tried hopelessly to staunch the spurting with his remaining hand. . . .

He drifted along beside Morga, who suddenly seemed very tense. The combatants stared at one another across a heap of dead and wounded where the wooden wall had failed.

Morga was reading her stone of dreams:

We will share the power equally between us. Bring your aunt and come to us before the storm arrives and your father steals our triumph. Only later did she ever wonder which father he meant. Because she knew this was a message from Flacchus. They'd communicated like this before.

"Can I trust you?" she said at the stone and she knew it was writing the words in his crystal where he stood across the field.

As much as I you was the reply.

Arturus saw the fat man up on the arch holding his own glossy black stone near his face. That was interesting. It distracted from the agony all around him which had already taken his mind off images of Morga nude and lascivious.

"What will we do?" she asked, glancing back at the storm mass that was already sweeping down the valley like mad surf into a channel.

Touch the two stones together while the fire being is drawn up from under the hill, from the molten depths, to consume the sacrifice and seal the jewels together with its heat which is like no other in this paltry age and then you and I shall become great. Ask your stone if I lie.

"Does he say truth?" she asked. They'd moved through the Roman ranks now.

Yes, wrote her stone, *there is truth in his sayings.*

She was anxious. Arturus noticed and thought how she was a girl, after all, and needed a man's firmness. Yes, such power would rest better with a man. No doubt of it.

He felt strong and full of energy. He looked back at the suffering men and felt the necessary detachment this time. He forced himself to look on as a man must.

He still wanted to press the aching angle of his ecstasy into her magical loins, perhaps more than ever. But the new idea was gathering force: he was meant to be master of these weapons. He was to be a great warrior, as she said. This was the call of his destiny.

Fixed on the inrush of ideas flaring up in the fires of imagination, he followed her like a sleepwalker. The men on both sides now watched in silence. The roar of the storm crashed down over them. Some faces were pale and uneasy among the Picts. The light was starting to go greenish-black. The sun was dimming. Bita understood that. An eclipse.

Of course, she thought.

Because she was starting to realize, gods or no gods, that the inexplicable was inexplicably ordered.

The Picts were falling to their knees in a wave and raising their arms to the sun. Even the Romans were impressed, falling back in awe, pointing at the sky.

She followed her son and slim Morga to the massive stone arch that straddled the rock-lined pit. Somehow, the eclipse gave her confidence: if there was order without there had to be order within.

There will be no more help from outside, Abram had told her. But, perhaps, the outside and the inside were the same.

The storm's first loose fingering puffed dust around

them in erratic little whirlwinds. The light was gradually failing.

When the Picts knelt, moaning as the moon's dark disc began to eat the sun and the churning wall of clouds and spitting lightning, rain and ripping hailburst suddenly loomed over them, Subius told Sira and Sidar to run for the shelter of a spilled wall of broken stone that bent with the road in a sharp curve around the shoulder of the hill.

"Duck behind there," he ordered. Gusts were already slashing runs of dust from the fields and slope. Where the central mass of the storm touched the ground, the surface was chewed to shreds and sucked up into a miles-wide cyclone. "Take him." Meaning Leitus.

But he shook Sira's hand away.

"No," he said. "I see my son and wife. We've all been drawn to this moment." Flashes of dim gold seemed to mirror the scrawls of sudden lightning so that he saw in fragments, sometimes not even having to smack the earth with his improvised staff.

So he and bulky Subius Magnus were at the opening in the palisade with the roaring at their backs about the time Morga, Bita, and Arturus reached the arch and well hole where Flacchus and his Roman guardsmen waited. There were five of them and they stood unnaturally still. Three had been victims of his juggling game when he'd arrived at their camp.

Bita's inner senses perceived thin strands like black sunrays reaching from his dreamstone and touching each shoulder's head like one-string marionettes. She felt they were hollowed-out flesh and blood machines. When Flacchus spoke, his voice seemed to echo unnaturally like the reverberations of pebbles tossed into a dry well.

"Quickly," he said, "before he steals our triumph."

"Yes," cried Morga, excited, clutching her crystal.

The fat man leaped down with a revolting kind of grace and landed lightly on the stone border of the pit.

He stared at them with eyes like holes. He kept his sphere near his mouth and extended a preternaturally long tongue and licked it as if it were a honey drop. His free hand tore away his already ragged toga until he stood there nude, sagging and pale in the failing, blood-colored eclipse light.

"Now," he said in that rattling voice.

"Yes," she repeated, stripping herself.

"No!" Arturus cried.

Is this disgusting beast going to touch her? he thought.

Bita was fighting the dizziness as the black pressure of the storm sucked at her strength again.

Morga touched Arturus.

"This is necessary," she told him. "Don't interfere."

Now the front slammed across the hilltop in a burst of dust and slap of advance rain. The vast wings of churning darkness beat around them. Claws of wind reached down.

Arturus was completely distracted by Morga's body, a long, lithe gleam in the dimming light, touched with sickly red as the sun was blotted over.

He thought how she ought to be kept quietly for his pleasure while he built an empire. The details were vague but the gist was the stone in his hands and armies at his bidding flailing out over the earth in blood and fire. She was too weak, he thought. He pictured her licking his body, kneeling between his legs.

The future was rich with possibilities. He was itching for action. The energy from the stones was affecting him. He felt it. Loved the feeling. He felt tall and vital and ready. He moved a step closer to her. Flacchus and Morga, holding the already interacting stones, were experiencing ten times the surging elevation that was lifting Arturus.

I'll strike him dead, Morga was thinking of Flacchus, *once the two are made one. . . .*

Arturus thought:

Wait and watch and then I'll take both of them. . . .

Subius took counsel with himself:

I don't like the look of this much. The trick will be to snatch up Bita and her son once they're all busy with whatever nonsense is about to unfold here. . . . He felt Sira and Sidar were safe for now. Unless this damned storm blows us all to destruction. . . . He wished he had a flask of wine to soothe him. Watched Bita swaying there behind her son and the slim girl and the grossly fat man who'd just taken off his clothes. He chose not to think about that. *She's falling. . . .*

But two Roman guards, with surprising speed, caught Bita from both sides. The bulk of the troops were about one hundred yards away, strung out around the perimeter except for those still concentrated near the breached wall. They and the Picts were just watching now as the storm crashed and the sun was swallowed up.

The two guards dragged Bita to the edge of the pit. That brought something back that fifteen years had blurred over. . . .

Leitus, blinking his dead eyes, suddenly reignited the golden fire and saw Bita in a halo of subtle monochrome, brighter than any of the others. The sky was beaten gold, the earth thickly molten, the churning clouds funneling down on the hill no color at all, the interacting dreamstones like three jet black holes, as if perfectly round pieces of reality had been cut out leaving a terrible void that twisted and pulled at his mind until he jerked his focus away. So while he was actually the second one to know there were really three stones there, it was only a glimpse and meant nothing to him yet. The golden sheen ran most details together, so he wasn't really sure Bita was in danger even though the shadows had suddenly closed around her.

The soldiers, moving stiffly but rapidly, suspended Bita over the opening. The manacles that hung from the center of the arch were fixed to her ankles. They left her swinging in the puffing gusts as the wall of storm leaned over them.

Arturus glanced up and noticed that a funnel-shaped swirl was dipping down like a vulture's beak from near the top edge of the cloud mass that was forming into something like the eye of a hurricane with the hilltop as the center.

When he looked down they'd just finished chaining up his mother. He was furious.

So they mean to defy me! he thought.

"We'll soon see about this!" he raged. "We'll soon see!"

He drew the dagger she'd given him. He was the master. Others would suffer!

Morga's arm was outstretched full-length, the stone pulling like a magnet towards the one in Flacchus' grip. He had positioned himself so that they were facing one another across the opening where Bita now hung just over their heads, upside down. She had an impression he was mocking her. Why? Why? What had she missed?

She flooded questions at the crystal.

Am I safe? What's his plan? Can I yet prevail?

But the red writing roiled meaninglessly. A few senseless fragments spun across the surface. *Blood undone fool fool fool all undone . . .*

And she realized she no longer had control of the stone. If, in fact, she ever really had.

And then she was dragged forward across the opening until the stones clacked together. The impact sent a shock up her outstretched arm. Her fingers were clamped around the smooth roundness and she realized she couldn't unlock her grip even if she'd wanted to.

There was a steady rush of heat in the shaft as if there were a smokeless blaze down below. She thought she could see winks and faint, distant flickers of flamelight down there. She was suddenly afraid.

"Help me, Arturus," she cried. "Quickly, help me!"

He was thinking this was the moment. Take both stones while they were stretched out naked and helpless. He had two hands: one for each.

• • •

Subius and Leitus braced against the wind. The dust and clouds billowed. The sun was darkened to a ghastly blood-colored smear.

Subius, bending close to Leitus, said:

"I'll free your wife. Then we'll run for it."

Leitus could see the golden smoothness around Arturus was stained with darkness.

Bita was partly conscious. Her head felt swollen with blood. She blacked out and came back over and over as she swung over the hole. Hot air poured up over her.

Upside down the sky became the cloudy, swirling earth and the heavens were a solid mass. She saw that the Picts and Romans had just been swept up, that they spun and danced together into the air with chunks of the palisade, shields, whole uprooted trees, gouts of earth, all circling around the center of the storm until they were sucked out of sight into the billowing fury above.

The beaklike tornado had nearly reached the arch as if to meet the uprush of heat in the shaft. She felt something coming up the shaft. Something dense and hot and terrible. Upside down, she saw Flacchus and Morga like two hopeless and parted lovers reaching desperately across the abyss for one final touch; where the two stones touched red curls and ripples burst into the tortured air. And now the clouds were closing in tighter and tighter.

The twisting, volatile minds trapped in the crystals were now spilling out into the mad atmosphere as the stones were suddenly shrinking, growing denser. Morga felt the new weight drag at her arm, her fingers locked to the shrinking ball of hardness. The red glare coming up the well was brightening and hot as a furnace.

She still kept trying to question the stone but there was nothing now but red and black chaos.

"Help me," she begged. "Please!"

She could see the fat Roman's face twisted in what seemed a leer of triumph and pleasure. She felt the terrific power of the third crystal though she didn't see it yet. She knew he had it now.

"Help me!"

The things that were Flacchus laughed:

"No help," he shouted over the still increasing wind. "All is mine." He leered up at the single fang of tornado that had almost reached them. "Too late," he taunted it. The thing that was Flacchus' desires flared up wildly and the world seemed to take new shapes. It leered at Bita, aware of the terror it had called from below, to devour her, the ancient creature that had been trapped under this sacred hill for ages, the stone-eater, the melter, called in the elder tongue, the Zug. A flat, skatelike creature that lived in rivers of molten stone, whose heat kept the rocks liquid.

The Flacchus thing was filled with earth's tortured memory of all brute things from the beginning; with deaths, pains, all suffering and furies and slow revenges and distorted desires. . . . The Flacchus thing knew that Bita's god-enhanced soul had drawn up the Zug, and that in its heat the stones would fuse together.

Morga was still trying to let go. She was screaming as the crystal shrank and crunched her hand bones pressed flat to the surface. Her screams were lost in the mounting tumult.

Morga glimpsed Flacchus, face a mask of hate and gloat and . . .

He dipped his head so that the redness blazed from his skull and joined the overlapping spray from the other two stones. He stared down, watching the molten light brightening below and the shadow of the rising Zug. She felt her arm was about to rip from the socket while black totality of eclipse sealed the gate to heaven's fire for the few minutes it would take to dim all the light in the world forever. . . .

Bita, the heat blasting into her face, the black beams

from the storm draining her vitality, the pounding blood dulling her upside-down head, lost consciousness. She fought but went under. She assumed she was doomed—except now there was a flicker, a deep spark far behind her eyes, an infinitely tiny jewel of golden flame and, as the mad, tormented, upside down world receded the pure fleck expanded into a sphere . . . wider . . . wider . . . until she sat on silvery gold grasses under a subtly fired sky like softly hammered golden leaf. Lustrous, thick, crumbly-looking blossoms spilled across the lucent fields, all tones of gold and hints of silver. Impossibly tall and slender trees rose here and there, the leaves bright shimmers that rang like tiny bells in the eternal afternoon. Everything was somehow weightless yet substantial. She stood up and floated slightly. Felt the color and atmosphere flowing around her naked body. Such joy and lightness. Existence glowed around her like a foam bubble. She was alone there and she understood what that meant. This was not an illusion nor was it the home of gods, though they might have come there if she'd called. This was the world in her heart. The world they all had to discover.

She wanted to dance across the rolling landscape toward the flashing ripples of distant water and steeper hills and gardens beckoning enchantment . . . she wanted to explore and see who and what might be waiting for her there. Lose herself in the mysterious and absorbing nooks and byways. It was no illusion. Neither was the voice that was her spirit speaking, and not the words of any god or spirit or dream this time. She knew now that while her body could die, this place, the center of herself, would remain forever. But the voice said she had to go back. Go back and help whoever she could help. *You have seen the world within. Leave the gate unlocked. Pull the coverings from the window and unbolt the door; leave it swinging wide. . . .*

And then she was back, rocking over the hot pit, clouds and hail-laced wind breaking over her. . . .

Now, thought Arturus, as the wind hit and he leaped

past the guards who'd made a tight cordon around the pit. They clutched at him but were shoved aside by the same violent gust that slammed him into the low wall.

He nearly went over but managed to catch himself and then clutch at both their hands. He made contact and something hit him like a dense electric pressure and he was flipped back upright as if shot from a catapult. He crashed into a solid bulk behind him that he assumed was one of the Romans.

It was Subius Magnus, a sword in his hands. Two of the guards lay headless at his feet. He brushed the boy aside, managed to jump up onto the bricked rim and brace himself long enough in the heat and wind fury to clamp one massive hand around Bita's knee and sacrifice his sword in an all-out chop that snapped the blade and both strands of chain that held her dangling. A moment later the tornado reached the top of the arch, sucking at them all, and next a massive, stonelike, dark, faceless flatness, dripping molten fires, thrashed up like an immense fish, lunging from the pit, the brick sides bursting into flame.

Leitus saw everything in a clear, calm golden glow. All the contorted fury of the storm was a wisping shadow in his strange vision.

He recognized his son beside him, gripping him to resist the wind.

"Artur," he called across the furious inches separating their faces. Touched him with his free hand. Arturus' eyes, to Leitus' senses, seemed pitted with dull whorls of shadow. He put his palm over the boy's forehead and for an instant the glow cleared like a rainpool when a cloud passes over.

"Father," he cried. Then the wind broke their contact and his gaze redarkened. "They're mine, Father," he yelled. "You cannot steal what is mine either!"

The forces spilling from the three crystals had created a whirlpool around the well more intense than the unnatural cyclone itself. The fragmented intelligences continued to be shrunk out of the diminishing spheres.

They blasted and twisted every mind in the vicinity except Leitus'; to his golden sight it was merely more vague ugliness like the pits in his son's eyes.

The madness of ages flooded through Morga, Flacchus, the five soldiers, and, to a lesser extent, Subius, Arturus, and Bita. The five soldier-puppets were rolling, chewing, ripping at the earth with fingers and teeth. Because their wills had already been dissolved, the insanity completely filled and animated them, a shattered madness now without the black sphere to give it a semblance of form and purpose. Howling ghosts of hate and longing sucked away into the winds of eternity.

Subius, clutching Bita, staggered and babbled, thinking in a senseless rush how he'd rape her, eat her flesh, kill everyone, make himself a king. Arturus was in a frenzy to take the stones, chewing his lips to bloody shreds. Moving like a demented machine with sudden power and skill far beyond his years and experience, twisted away the sword his father had been using as a cane, whirled with it upraised and drawn, froze a fraction as half a dozen lightning bolts from the blinding clouds smashed into the blade and left it glowing like a fallen star and still in the same motion reached the well rim and screamed "Mine! Mine! Mine!" just as the sluglike thing burst from the pitmouth, dripping molten fire. Hands locked together by the fusing dreamstones, the naked Roman and slim Morga staggered back from the burst of heat. The Flacchus thing was shocked and furious because it had been certain it had the power to restrain the Zug's energy and focus it on the three crystals to make them one.

The Zug beat back and forth in the melting, flaming opening like a hooked fish. Arturus hit it with the shining blade that was the only real brightness at the dark bottom of the storm. The creature fell back from the impact; the tornado hung now a few feet above the arch.

"Mine!" Arturus howled again. Turned and slashed at Flacchus' wrist where he and Morga stood braced against the wind in a parody of holding hands. Flacchus jerked back and the cut took off Morga's hand instead. The two stones were partly melted into one and her fingers remained clenched. She fell sideways, wrist stump spilling blood spatters.

She paid no attention to her wound, scrambling desperately around the well, seared by the molten rock that hissed and flew as the Zug thrashed, thwarted. She clawed for Flacchus with her remaining hand.

"Thief!" she yelled. "Thief!"

The Flacchus thing saw one last hope. The Zug had dropped back down to whatever pool of flame it existed in, but the stones were half fused and still radiating. It raised the two to its mouth which stretched, gaped abnormally wide as if the skull were bending open, small bones snapping, a vomitus of icy blackness seeming to pour from its face that was all mouth now, eyes, nose squashed and wrinkled away, about to swallow the stones, Morga's fingers and all, as if they were two crystal eggs.

"Me!" the gaping howled. "Me!"

Except Arturus staggered down the three steps against the gale and brought down the flaming sword again. The terrible mouth flung black spew, with casual scorn, to block the blade. The willforce of that concentrated plurality should have checked a falling mountain.

There was absolutely no pause in the blow. The arc hit the mouth and smashed the skull in two. Except the sword glanced off something solid. And then Arturus saw the third stone was actually inside the skull. It had replaced Flacchus' brain. The blow had cracked it, cracked a substance no blow had ever before dented or scratched. Only Bita and the Hebrew seers at that time knew that the sword had been forged long before even those crystal globes of darkness. That sword had been created by the Avalonians at the height of their glory. It was meant to alter human history and pierce the armor of Lord Ata himself.

Cracked, the dreamstone folded in on itself, bent time and space into a black blossom where the head had just been. The body, instead of falling, was sucked up into the blossom and vanished. Even the incredible storm paused and the ground trembled—as if heaven and earth knew, Bita was to think later, that history had just been changed.

And then there was nothing there. Just an echo of wailing as all the trapped souls blew away. The other two globes, shrunk to twin marbles now and half melted together, had fallen beside the well. The shattered, melted brickwork was cooling in the wind and rain.

Arturus stood there, swaying, nothing in his hands but a hilt and bladestump. The swirling madness was gone. Blown away. Morga had been blown flat, clutching her ruined arm.

His heart sank.

What have I done? his mind cried.

To his father's vibrant unsight there was a rent in the golden perfection of the world. He looked up at it. In the center of the vaster cyclone the tornado pointed straight down at the pit. To Leitus there was something solid and dark there. Something disturbing and familiar. He watched and waited now, crouched against the jerking of the gale.

Subius, holding Bita under one arm, was moving blindly in the tattered blackness of cloud and eclipse. He hunched almost to his knees. Couldn't see three feet in any direction. Dust and pebbles, rain and hailstones stung him.

Bita was aware, though her body stayed limp. Nothing, she now knew, would ever obliterate her consciousness. The other world would always be there untouched, unshaken. . . .

Riding ahead of the fringe of the main fury as it closed on the hill, spinning in a kind of dance, mad Arim Ben Ymir had run and been blown up over the crest. He believed the wind was divine and was filling him with truth and just wrath. He saw the evil forming over the pit and knew his moment had come. Knew he would redeem the blindness of all Israel. Saw the enemy's form shrouded in the dense fogs of greed and ignorance and misbelief.

He went forward as if his movements had been rehearsed a dozen times. He rushed on the wind to meet the enemy, paying scant attention to the lost souls he saw in thrall there. They would soon be free. . . .

Arturus watched Flacchus shrivel, float, then fold into the void where his head had been, a flapping sack of pale, loose flesh, gone instantly.

He tossed the hilt aside and dove over to her.

"I'm sorry," he told Morga. She clung to him. The tornado funnel just above them forced him to grip the hot wall to keep them both on the ground.

"My son," said Leitus into the overwhelming wind. Subius, holding Bita like a child in his arms, was desperately hunkering away.

Now something massive and angular seemed to be sliding down the miles-long funnel, bulging it out until, near the base, it burst into a towering, winged, impossibly massive figure that only Bita actually recognized. Leitus, who'd fought it face-to-face fifteen years before in the red and black underworld, didn't see it except as a stress of shadow in the clear golden sheen, so he didn't really see Aataatana, upheld by twisting, primal energies, hovering in person on the wings of his dread science. The force of his presence seemed to tilt the scene like the deck of a pitching vessel. His long, slanted eyes were blank red flame burning through the enveloping tornado that supported him. One taloned hand reached down, wrapped in boiling fury, clawing at the two remaining dreamstones that Flacchus had dropped, Morga's fingers still crumpled around one. . . .

The wind had rolled and spilled Arim Ben Ymir across the flat hilltop. He narrowly missed cracking into one of the standing stones. At last he was closing with the enemy. He was on all fours now, scuttling sidewise against the wind, almost at the pit when Ata took form in the tortured air.

This was his moment and God's voice seemed to speak out of the wind's wail:

The evil one, it seemed to say, *must taste My wrath*.

"Yes," he responded, "and I am Thy flail and the hammer of Thy fury, O Lord God!"

So he charged for the immense floating figure with perfect confidence, like a crazed sparrow toward a hunting hawk.

Bita, though paralyzed, watched everything through her inner sense, through the light of her heart. She saw Subius holding her as he reeled and crawled blindly against wind blasts under the blocked sun and massed clouds that seemed to have absorbed all light forever. She perceived the dread figure suspended above them, reaching to gather his last two lost jewels, his stare like slits in a furnace door. She glimpsed the mad Jew scampering to the attack, shouting words that were blotted from his mouth by the cyclone. She watched her eyeless husband trying to save their son.

She winced inwardly as the ruby-tipped claws snapped closed over the fused black stones—except the Jew dove between the spidery fingers in a skinny flash and snatched the stones away.

He shouted:

"I have them, O Lord, even the testicles of the evil one that he may no longer spread his seed of misery and ignorance. . . ."

The myriad minds still trapped in the stones were spinning in shock and confusion because the third had died blasting them into greater frenzy than before, because, slowly but steadily, the dreamstones continued to shrink.

"This is his poison and his delight," Ben Ymir called out in triumph as the dense claws ripped into him. He flopped and spun in a spray of blood. Still holding the stones, he toppled over the rim into the well. The giant glossy hand slammed and shattered the bricks, trying to squeeze the huge fist down the shaft.

Only Bita glimpsed what happened next in the heart of that terrible darkness. The shredded body of Ben Ymir fell on top of the wounded Zug. Her heartsense saw the flat, eyeless, earless, faceless thing blast his flesh to cinders and ignite the stones. Then there was just a blur as a shock wave burst out of the well mouth, the impact driving Ata aside. The storm collapsed down, crashing back into its own center and the Zug fell out of sight. . . .

Arim Ben Ymir felt the claws slice him but still was suffused with joy, gripping the doubled stones as he sailed down the shaft. The brightness of molten rock below him he perceived as angelic glory. He heard music, a singing brightness, the swirling glory of the seven heavens under God's downpouring benediction . . . as his dying senses and nerves, overloaded by the dissolving dreamstones, burst into spectral and supernal light.

Aataatana screamed in flame. His crashing fists kept smashing the arch and well rim into a spray of broken stone. Arturus rolled with Morga in his arms trying to avoid the hammer blows. Rock chips cut them. The earth shook. The storm was imploding. He got his feet under him in the raging, utter blackness and staggered with her. The wrong way, because there was ground, wind, impacts and then nothing but a sickening rush down and he knew he'd blundered into the shaft.

Bita cried out soundlessly within herself in terrible anguish. The storm had gone completely dead. It had become a static, smoky pall of darkness.

O my son, she thought. *O my job . . .*

Leitus had been knocked flat by a near miss. The shock of Ata's blow had flipped him into Subius and Bita. The atmosphere was a sooty wall, dense and hard to breathe.

He reached out and took Subius' hand.

I understand now, he said to himself. *I understand what had to be . . . the flesh is nothing but a rag and the light is everywhere. . . .*

He was walking through a landscape of softened gold, each tree, each blade of grass or spiky flower stalk, each stirring creature a rich glow, the sky like music. He led Subius down the slope toward Sira and Sidar who were wandering, frantic, groping through the radiant landscape that to them was black, strangling air. He felt sadness and pity for them mixed with joy. To move, exist in such beauty and yet not know it. . . .

He felt his wife's love like the pressure of sunbeams on his soul. Despite the loss of Arturus he felt hope. There wasn't time to grieve yet and maybe there was no reason. He'd see what all that meant in time.

"By Hermes," Subius was saying in the deadening silence, "the air is thick and cold and sickening to breathe."

Their voices were muffled and flat, as if they were struggling at the bottom of a lightless sea.

Then Sira's voice, and Sidar's:

"Help us! Help . . . Where are you?"

"Mother . . . I'm afraid, Mother . . . I can't see anything, Mother. . . ."

"Stay still. Where are you, child? Stay still," her mother responded in near panic because Sidar had lost her grip and had wandered, Leitus saw, two steps away on the glory of the soft-tinted field into slight shifts of subtle illumination. He almost laughed, for a moment, to see them groping amidst such bright perfection.

"Here," he said. He reached and joined their hands again. "Follow me," he said. "Hold me."

"Sira," Subius said, Bita still slung across his back.

"Subius?" Sira asked. "Where?" Then she found him and clutched him. "What?"

"I know not," the ex-gladiator answered, "but Leitus is leading us."

Into a wall of night, yet denser than night or fog. Heaven and earth were utter black. The defeat of

Aataatana had left the world opaque.

They strung out behind Leitus, each touching each, as he headed towards the coast on a road that ran through fields alive with the mingling, shimmering golden tones of all that lived there, the human colors spreading out, fanning into the landscape. Leitus had difficulty concentrating on anything but the delight of this walk that was such a choking terror to the others.

"It will soon pass," he assured them. Why, he couldn't have explained, but he knew he was right. "Just follow me." He knew Bita would be all right. He could feel her love.

There was nothing but falling. Nothing on any side, above or below. Arturus saw her in front of him, falling. Something like slow, thick atmosphere suspended them. There were no walls to the pit. Only falling without end.

I hate you, she somehow said. There was no sound, yet he heard her voice.

I'm sorry I hurt you, he responded.

I hate you; you ruined it all you . . . you . . .

I'm sorry, I'm sorry, I'm sorry. . . .

In dread, they fell into nothingness that was gray and dim, not even quite lightless.

I'll never forgive you, she somehow told him.

Please, he reacted, spinning slowly behind her into the endless gray. *Please, Morga . . .*

No, she told him.

They fell, slowly turning, down into what wasn't even down and had no bottom.

Never, she told him. *Never. . . .*

Elsewhere, on the open sea, under a coppery brightening afternoon sky, Naiar was watching the shadow gradually passing over the sun. He sat alone on the deserted, burnished, water-smooth deck of the gilded royal barge, the emptied pouch of forgetfulness drugs open and empty in his lap.

He stared, eyes tracking the brightening water. The

wind shook the bunched, uneven sails. The waves smacked the hull. He stared in wordless wonder, because words were the first things he'd forgotten. Wondered what all these things were. Now and then he'd grip his bare toes with curious fingers, pulling and wondering, rolling from side to side on the smooth wood with the slight pitching of the ship.

Now and then he felt discomfort in his body that he didn't know was hunger. His smooth face would wrinkle up, eyes squinting, a squalling, wordless call would well up and break from his mouth, a cry of frantic desperation. . . .

Below deck the queen still sat rocking slightly at her table. The masses of gold wrapped around her body clinked with the vessel's rhythm.

Marc Antony's corpse lay at her bare, jeweled feet, the short, thick Roman blade driven up under his sternum. The blade, too, swayed with the deck's slight tilts.

A stray thread of reddish sunlight, going gradually gold as the eclipse ended, poked down into the twilight gloom through a space in the planking. It touched the blade and reflected soft chips of light over Antony's relaxed face, over and over, keeping nature's perfect and unsemantic time.

And, as in a dark dream, Antony stood in the bow of a long, low, jet black boat that was crossing black water toward a shore of shadows. A river coastline, massive, without detail.

He was chilled and full of grief. He kept feeling sighs that made no sound in his mouth. Nothing there made any sound. Though he'd lost her name he knew her, remembered, and without sound grieved and wanted . . . wanted . . . ah, wanted!

And then the boat, the ferry, was gone, and he was in the water. Had he been tripped out? By who or what? He'd already swallowed a mouthful and numbness rose and began washing away the dry sands of his grieving thoughts and hopeless longing to go back, to find her, because there was no back, no finding. . . . So it was mercy to forget and swallow the river's icy, numbing draughts . . . because it was all lost, walled away by forever, and finally her face, like a sketch in the sands, blurred and washed away too. . . .

He was just an outline to himself now, an outline in the dark flow of eternal water. A rim, a hinting . . . his thinking was washed away, everything, and yet something not him and not words and not anything was explaining:

You will have to return. You will see her again, though it will not be her and you will not be you, yet shall you meet again. . . .

His empty outline drifted on the lightless river, a faint, luminous tracing . . . floating away. . . .

EPILOGUE

Just before they reached the cliffs that fell away to the channel beaches the thick, strange clouds simply ended: One step Subius, just behind Leitus, hand clasped to hand, was in total darkness, the next he was looking out over a sparkling sheet of water under a hot, brilliant sun.

Almost immediately, Bita stirred in his arms.

"Mother," Sidar said, as they followed her farther into the sunshine. They were gathered on a strip of green that ran along the rocky cliff top. There were puffs of bushes there with winks of red and violet, tiny flowers.

"Thank Isis," said her mother.

Subius set Bita on her feet. She didn't quite reel. Her tattered, weather-stained robes were more gone than present. Subius looked back and up at the sheer wall of sooty blackness that the breezes seemed to undulate more like a fabric than smoke or fog.

"You could just about lay a measuring rod along the edge," he said.

Bita shook herself and stiffly moved her limbs. Leitus was embracing her.

"My dearest one," he said.

She held him. Basked in him. It seemed to him he was holding a radiance, an outspraying of golden light. And, to her, he was closer than her skin, touching her heart which was a world where they both stood in a perfect and timeless landscape and nothing would ever have to be said about it.

"Our son," he murmured.

"I know," she replied, holding him. "I know. I saw too."

"You saw?"

"Yes."

"I felt you."

"I know." She kissed his neck like a butterfly's weightless flutter.

"Our poor son," he said.

"No," she said. "He wasn't destroyed. No more than you are blind, my husband."

"Will we meet him again do you think?"

"Not for some time, Leitus."

Subius poked his arm into the black wall. As much as went in simply disappeared and felt cold. He shook his head.

"What a thing," he said.

"Will it go away?" Sidar wanted to know.

"What is it?" Sira asked. Then turned and looked across the brilliant water. "It was terrible. I thought we were dying in there."

Bita looked at them, one hand touching Leitus.

"I don't see what you're talking about," he told her.

"Then you are blessed, my husband," Bita responded. She was thinking about when they'd first met at his uncle's when she was a slave. His uncle who had been Flacchus before the dark swirlings took him over and amplified his own desires and greeds and ended by replacing his brain with a stone. She remembered how she'd loved him first when she was thirteen and he never noticed. She'd never stopped. "It is a taste of the world they hoped to create." She sighed. "It took my strength away, yet I lived in it."

"That was important," he agreed. It was, because all these symbols were real too. They would change the world. Open the human heart.

"I don't understand this thing," Subius pursued.

"Who could?" Sira asked. "I want to go away from here. I know not how I came or why, but I surely want to leave. I was better off in that miserable tavern."

"Fear not," Subius assured her. "We'll go." Then, to Leitus and Bita: "And a blind man led us to safety." He raised his eyebrows and planted his big hands on his hips. "I think I need no more of you, Leitus. No more. I couldn't survive another dose."

Leitus half smiled. It was not, he decided, even half amusing.

"Then don't follow me any farther," he said.

His eyes, Subius noted, were raw squints. But Subius knew the man could see him. How he'd changed since those first days when he'd been a spoiled, fearful, arrogant Roman medical student. Then Subius had turned him into a gladiator, and Caesar had turned him into a soldier, and things unknown into something stranger still. . . . He knew he was going to keep following him. The question was only *why*.

"To where," Subius asked, "am I not to follow?"

Bita understood at once.

"They will be back to try again and again," she said. "We have to ready ourselves to deny them or else all the earth will be shrouded." She gestured at the black wall. "Like this. And worse still."

"Where?" repeated Subius.

"To Judea," Leitus answered. He knew that was right. The radiance was brighter than the sun he could not actually see. And there were purposes and directions in it. Direction. A way. His own words seemed to be discovered out of the shining.

"Yes," said Bita, graceful, delicate, indestructible as wind and the reflowering of every springtime. "The Devil has lost his seed. And Jehova, Lord God, is preparing his own planting."

"Seed?" Sidar wondered. She looked doubtfully at the blackness looming, unmoving, high over them, unaffected by the hot sun—except it might have been just starting to shrink, she noticed. "Like planting grain?"

"Which god?" put in Sira. "The Jewish one?"

"Everybody's," Bita told her.

"But," persisted the young girl.

"Say it's a jewel then," Bita answered her. "Not like a seed at all. Say he's giving us a jewel brighter than the sun. Say that."

"A real jewel?" Sidar wondered, interested. "How much would it cost?"

Leitus had started moving, picking his way rapidly down the jagged cliff face, smoothly, without hesitation.

"You'll be able to afford it," Bita told her, smiling, turning to go after her husband.

"Follow me," he called up. "I swear, Subius, that only a blind man will be of any use to you from this day on."